pack light, travel light, be the light

tiffany manchester

Copyright

pack light, travel light, be the light

Tish, 23, freshly home from Africa is already seeking her next adventure. She is sick of the city, the tight grip of mainstream society, and her disapproving parents. There has to be more people like her out there. But who are they? And where?

Desperate to find her people, she heads out into the Canadian wilderness where she discovers the thrill of being on the river and the challenge of navigating whitewater armed only with a paddle and her fellow rafters. Little does she know it will be the spark lighting the way to new, often harrowing adventures.

Along with her constant companion Red Fran, she finds herself avoiding death on her moped in Taipei, getting lost hiking the Annapurna Circuit in Nepal, being stuck in the jungle in Ecuador for three days with nothing but two mangos and a bottle of rum, and tackling the craziest rapid yet in Uganda... as well as finding the love of her life.

But the biggest adventure of all? Having to face her true Self, and her fears, every step of the way.

———

"OMG I just finished your book and I absolutely loved it. Like really really really loved it. It's as good as The Way Of The Peaceful Warrior!" - Michelle Melendez

"A crazily relatable and inspiring story that caused me to reflect on the concept of courage and how I can relate it to my own life." - Ruby Meade

also by tiffany manchester

Surfacing

Zoe Smith is flailing in her career as a professional surfer on the WSL (World Surf League)...as well as in her relationship with Derek. She needs to make a change. But what?

Stuck in a funk, she heads home to Australia at the end of the competitive season, uncertain of her future. Will the end of her relationship also signify the end of her career, or will her life take a turn for the better?

Luckily, with the help of a best friend, a boy crush, a strange encounter with an angel, and some much-needed soul-searching, she finds herself on a magical journey out of the darkness and into the light...in surfing and in life.

part i

looking for a new adventure

· · ·

June 1996

I WAS desperate to get out of the house and checking the bulletin board at Mountain Equipment Co-op (MEC) was as good a reason as any. It was my mom's suggestion. Maybe she was sick of watching me mope around like a lost soul. Being stuck at home had been doing my head in. I hated the rigidity of the city when the sun was shining and it felt even more constricting this summer after returning from my adventures in Africa.

I loved MEC. It was big and beautiful and could fulfill every outdoor adventure fantasy. I had spent a great deal of time there prior to my Africa trip, and as I walked through those giant automatic sliding doors, I was once again hit with the nervous anticipation that I had felt all of those months prior.

I remembered picking out the purple sleeping bag that would keep me warm during the month we would spend climbing Mt. Kenya, and finding the perfect hiking boots that I was instructed to break in at home so that I could cross the mountain blister-free. I remembered choosing the transparent Nalgene water bottle (instead of the opaque one) that I went on to use to filter some thick brown water as we hiked through the scorching hot and unbearably dry landscape of the Maasai Mara; the Swiss Army knife I used to slice through many a delectable mango as we

3

sailed on a traditional *dhow* through the Lamu Archipelago, and proudly choosing last season's backpack because its price was heavily discounted.

This beautiful red backpack had been my constant companion.

I'd named her Red Fran.

Africa was not an inexpensive trip. Even though I'd worked two jobs for the five months prior to my departure to help fund it, I was also fortunate enough to have parents willing and able to split the cost with me. They may not have been eager about my choice of destination. (My mom had said at the time with tears in her eyes, "Oh Tish, if anything ever happened to you...") They had never gotten in my way, either. They always supported me and my sister as best they could.

My parents loved to travel too, so it made complete sense to me that we would also inherit their adventurous spirit.

My upbringing was one of privilege, and though we never had the white picket fence, we always had a pool, and even a tennis court. I attended a private girls' school. We had a summer cottage in the Muskokas, a winter chalet in Collingwood, and every spring break, we traveled somewhere new, be it a ski trip in France, a visit to Hollywood, or a tour of Italy. I went on an Australian exchange program when I was 16 and then spent a semester in Nice, France at 18. But the absolute best part of my childhood was getting to spend every July at summer camp. It was there I had the most fun.

I may have *acted* like a spoiled brat on more occasions than I care to remember, but I wouldn't say I was spoiled. My dad made sure I wasn't blind to the opportunities given to me, making me work for my allowance and such, wanting me to understand the value of money.

All in all, I consider myself lucky that my parents felt it important to show us the world and shower us with opportunity so we could see for ourselves what was out there. It fueled the fire within me, and the more I saw, the more I wanted to see.

it's my choice to be free
choose my path as I please
it's safe to be me
that's how I feel most at ease.

Since my return, with all my excited talk of seeking more adventure, something had shifted. I no longer felt my parents' support. Apparently, they thought Africa was my last hurrah. Now that I was 23, I should be getting on with my life and making use of my useless degree, the BA that everyone had told me I needed, but I was realizing I couldn't actually do anything with. At the very least, I was meant to be finding an acceptable job. In their eyes, anyway.

For me, it was the opposite. I was *only* 23 and just getting started!

After five months of traveling Africa, I could tell my mom wasn't keen for me to jump on yet another outrageous adventure so quickly. She was still recovering from the emotional toll of me doing a semester in Kenya with NOLS (National Outdoor Leadership School), and then backpacking solo down to South Africa via Tanzania, Malawi, and Zimbabwe. Once in Cape Town, I had planned to either stay and work there for the summer, or go back up to Zimbabwe to become a whitewater rafting guide. But after tearing some ligaments in my knees after an awkward landing while cliff-jumping, I was forced to return home to Toronto.

Mom had been suffering from migraines since the day I'd left, and at one point she'd even gone for an MRI, worried that perhaps she had a tumor. But the scans had come back clear, and upon my return home, the migraines immediately disappeared. I only knew this because my dad had enthusiastically shared this story at the dinner table, mocking her sarcastically.

"David!" she interrupted him, unimpressed. I guess she didn't want me to know what she had gone through.

Such is a mother's worry. On the one hand, it was annoying, but I do get it. I was only able to contact them via collect calls in international phone booths at various points on my journey, which amounted to once or twice per month. Each time I could feel how stressed she was by the tone of her voice.

"Tish! Tish! Are you okay? Where are you? David! David! Pick up the phone, it's Tish!"

Only after I explained my whereabouts and insisted everything was fine would she calm down, but all that time between calls left too much to her imagination.

My dad always played it cool, but I knew he was concerned too. He never failed to ask if I had enough traveler's checks, which was his way of taking care of me. In his mind, if I had enough money, I would be fine. It was the one thing he could control.

But if I'd learned anything in Africa, it wasn't control...

what happened in africa

. . .

ANYWAY, back to Africa. So much had happened on that trip and because of it I was forever changed. The cultures, the experiences, the sights, the sounds, the tastes… Every day was new, always eye-opening, sometimes jaw-dropping and occasionally death-defying.

The Maasai people, with their stretched earlobes and red patterned robes (though Robert, one of our Massai guides, wore a white bed sheet adorned with pretty pink flowers), refer to us as 'O Lo Lani' meaning 'foreign travelers with luggage looking for trouble' in Kiswahili. It's an appropriate name. We carry all of our valuables and are obvious targets for getting robbed. They also call us the 'sexless turtles' because we wear baggy clothes with hats and carry backpacks so they can't tell who's male or female. This, coincidentally, helped us to understand why the topless Maasai women would just come up and put their hands on our chests. They were feeling for boobs.

The Maasai are a semi-nomadic people living under a communal land management system where the boys are responsible for herding livestock, the warriors in charge of security, and the men responsible for fencing the *kraal* (small neighborhood) with a circular fence made from acacia thorns. This prevents lions from attacking the cattle.

We slept in our other guide Richard's *boma* (hut), next to 30 goats separated only by a thin grass wall. I listened to the goats peeing and rubbing their asses against the wall all evening while trying not to choke on the smoke from the firepit five feet away from me. Richard's wife slept on the floor next to the fire, keeping it going. That was one of her jobs, as well as collecting wood, supplying water, milking cattle, cooking for family, and constructing these bomas made of mud, sticks, grass, cow dung, and cow urine.

We met a variety of young boys during our daily hikes, all of them with burn marks covering their arms. When I asked why, they replied it was practice for their next rite of passage… circumcision.

Circumcision took place at 15 years old. During the procedure, they would not be allowed to move or show any emotional expression. If they were to show emotion, it would bring shame upon their family. So they trained for it. Starting from a young age, Maasai boys practiced the art of physical and emotional control by burning themselves.

We were honored to be allowed to attend this ceremony, an event where *mzungus* (white people or Europeans), and especially women, were strictly forbidden. The privilege we had in witnessing first hand this ancient tradition was not lost on me. And whether or not there was a moral issue around it was not for me to judge. I was only there to observe.

> **feel the gentle breeze**
> **of your inner beliefs**
> **let them come**
> **then let them go**
> **your beliefs are not the real you**
> **so there's no need to carry them along with you.**

We sat cross-legged in the dirt at the back of the gathering, watching in quiet awe as one boy came out of a boma to the right. He walked as if in a trance. A bucket of water was then dumped on him before he was sat on the ground cover next to the hunched medicine man. I'm guessing the water was a symbol of purification or maybe to remove dirt, perhaps both.

The boy sat motionless; eyes closed with his arms behind his back. He had been preparing for this for years.

With an audience of about 50 tribe members, plus the ten of us travelers, the medicine man began. Wielding what looked from afar like an old paring knife, he circumcised the boy in one fell swoop. I was too far away to see what happened to his member in any detail, only that the boy didn't budge, blink or wince.

He stood up; his face showing no emotion. He held his penis in hand, now wrapped in a blood-soaked cloth, and not two minutes after he had entered, he retreated to the boma to the left where he would heal for a few days.

Not a moment later, the next boy appeared from the hut on the right.

After 30 minutes, 12 boys had become men.

While they rested, the celebrations started. Maasai from around the area had come to witness, then celebrate, all adorned in their signature beaded necklaces and earrings. While the elders got drunk on honey beer, the young Maasai males would do their warrior 'jumping' dance, leaping into the air from a standing position, a demonstration of strength and agility.

The way that they leapt into the air with zero momentum, I was sure I was witnessing some sort of superhuman power only available to these warriors.

The morning before the ceremony, we had purchased a goat as a celebratory meal for our guides, Richard and Robert, and their families. It was our contribution as a group, as well as a symbol of our gratitude for being included in this very sacred event.

So here we were, gathered around a campfire in the late afternoon after an exciting day. I gazed out at the arid land in the distance, awestruck at how *this* culture and *western* culture existed at the same time. And when the sun's heat began to loosen its grip, Robert brought the small goat over to us.

It was still alive.

the goat

. . .

ROBERT PULLED OUT A KNIFE. The goat, sensing danger, tried to resist, but a split second later, his throat was slit. Initially it stomped its feet while we all sat there, mouths agape. As the blood drained cleanly from his throat into a cup held steady in place by Richard, a slow and silent death ensued.

It was a lot of blood for one day, and this goat thing was emotionally challenging, because I wasn't just a witness to it, but partly responsible for it. Nevertheless, I was forced to remind myself that I was honored to be a part of this world for a short time. And for a minute or two, I truly felt I was. That is until Richard held out the cup to me and insisted I drink some of the blood.

"For courage!" he beamed.

Surely, the two guides must be joking. They *were* quite the jokesters. But they insisted they were serious, demonstrating it by happily drinking from the cup themselves, before trying to pass it off to me once again. Apparently, this was common practice for the leader, the one who kills the goat. And even though the goat hadn't been killed by my own hand, I had, unfortunately, been voted in as leader of our NOLS group for the next month, and I guess that was good enough for them.

I turned and walked away briskly, hoping to escape the peer pressure, but they, in their humor, chased me around with this cup, taunting me until I finally caved in. Despite my vegetarianism, there was no escaping this, I realized. I stopped and took the cup from Richard. Looking into it, I understood that the time I had spent avoiding the inevitable had only made things worse because, by this point, the blood had coagulated into a thick, dark red blob.

Fuuuuuck.

be bold
be brave
be your best YOU.

All eyes were on me. The others in my group thought this was the best thing ever, chanting my name louder and louder. I held my breath, reached in, and picked up this disgusting gelatinous lump of blood from the cup with two fingers, and with the tips of my teeth took a very shy bite.

Everyone cheered.

I grimaced.

They laughed.

I swallowed.

Salty. Tasted like metal.

I handed back the cup and ran off immediately to brush my teeth and mouth five times over while I heard everyone laughing in the distance. It was no use. I swear that tin-like salty flavor lasted for days.

Robert and Richard proceeded to butcher the goat with precision, sticking parts of the goat meat onto kebab sticks, making a sort of pyramid around the fire to roast the meat. The organs were boiled, the skin laid out to dry.

We sat by the fire under the stars and next to a large baobab tree, enjoying a special meal with our Maasai warrior guides while they shared stories of their lives. Despite my recent trauma of the goat blood and the meat being tough and flavorless, it was the most delicious culinary experience I'd ever had.

———

The legendary trip blew open my mind and gave me new perspective.

Yet adjusting to life back home, where the people around me were still sharing the same gossip from before I left, became even more of a challenge. These conversations I once thought interesting I now saw as empty small talk, devoid of any real life. And while I didn't know the future, I knew for sure that the city and the nine-to-five rat race was not something I could stomach. I absolutely would not succumb to its mind-numbing tendencies.

Even when I visited my sister at her office, I could feel my soul being sucked out of me as I entered the building. I couldn't stick it out for five minutes in her cubicle before having to bolt. To me, all I saw was a trap.

But what *was* my next destination? Where would I go from here?

the sign of alignment

. . .

I STARED at the bulletin board with curiosity and cluelessness as to what I needed to see. There was a ride-share board for people looking to drive across the country. *Ooh, that could be fun.* A move to British Columbia? Or Alberta? I loved the idea of Canmore…

There were job postings for some retail and bartending jobs. Well, I certainly needed a job, but that wasn't gonna happen. Then my eyes wandered over to the brochure section where I noticed a bunch of different pamphlets for whitewater rafting.

"What? There's whitewater rafting? Here in Ontario?"

The hair on my arms stood on end. One of the brochures in particular caught my eye: River Run Rafting. The logo seemed familiar. But how? I'd never been to the Ottawa Valley before…

I picked up the brochure and flipped through it, enticed by the idea of becoming a raft guide. After all, hadn't that been one of my (many) ideas for how to stay and work in Africa? My mind, full of recent memories from that trip, wandered to the time I spent in Victoria Falls in Zimbabwe.

After the Kenya NOLS trip, most everyone went straight home, which I found surprising. Who would go all the way to the African continent and only see Kenya? Since I had booked my flight into Nairobi and out of Johannesburg, I had no choice but to journey south towards South Africa.

First, I took an overnight bus to Tanzania and then a ferry to Zanzibar where I relaxed and enjoyed the sun and Caribbean-type vibe. Then it was Malawi, a curiously kind place where men on bicycles taxi people across the border and males young and old walk together hand in hand. It was the sweetest thing. From there, I hitched a ride with an older Afrikaner bloke in his topless jeep all the way to Zimbabwe. We were stopped repeatedly by the corrupt police where my new driving friend would inevitably have to pay them off with a pack of cigarettes. It was a solid month from the time I left Kenya to the time I arrived in Zimbabwe and set up camp at the town of Victoria Falls.

How I longed to be there again now! There, where I bungeed 82 meters from the Victoria Falls bridge that crosses the Zambezi River and acts as the border between Zimbabwe and Zambia.

I loved this town for many reasons, but mostly because its local raft guides flirted with me incessantly. In particular, there was Frank, a safety kayaker who convinced me to go back to his place for breakfast one morning along with Kudzi and Steve, a couple of other raft guides I met while hanging out at Shearwater, the whitewater rafting office. I didn't have plans for the day, so against my better judgment, I figured I might as well go for it.

The thing about being a solo, white, female traveler in Africa is that you have to be careful. Of course, this is true wherever you go, but here, maybe a little bit more so. On multiple occasions, I'd had the experience that men wanted to either follow me or marry me, and so I had learned to watch my back, to be alert at every moment. In other words, I had to worry night and day about being robbed, harassed, or raped. It was discomforting. I hated that I only felt relief and security in the presence of other, particularly male, travelers.

But none of that had stopped me. On the contrary, I hopped in a taxi with these big, beautiful, strange men. As we headed to their living quarters, I tried desperately to memorize each turn we made in case I needed to make a run for it, but I lost my bearings on the third turn, killing any attempt at an emergency exit plan.

All I could do now was trust, and have faith that all would be well.

> keep the faith when you're afraid
> don't let darkness lead you astray
> why not face it with courage
> and ask 'hey, what would you say?'
> now listen with love...
> and feel how these ghosts fade away
> hooray! the light has come
> it's here to stay.

It started out okay. They made scrambled eggs and screwdrivers, we played frisbee on the back lawn, and the whole time, Frank was a blatant flirt. I felt fine around him. But when Frank went inside the house, the other two started fighting over me as though I was a toy.

"No. Steve, you had the last one. I am not doing this again."

"You lie. She is for me."

I bolted.

In a different circumstance, I may have enjoyed watching this altercation, but as it stood, I was tipsy and fatigued from the screwdriver and could feel my dark imaginings getting the best of me. Maybe it was my intuition. I don't know. Either way, I headed down the street, hoping I was going in the right direction.

"Tish, Tish!"

Frank caught up to me. I didn't even hear his footsteps until he had called out my name and was already a mere five feet behind me.

"Hey," I said.

"Why did you leave? I'm sorry about those two. They are stupid. Please, I will walk you back."

He took my hand in his, and from the confidence of his grip I could tell he wasn't going to take no for an answer. Ever so forward, these men. I was secretly relieved he was walking me back to town, since I didn't know where I was going. When we got there, he left for the rafting headquarters while I went back to the campground to take a nap.

I hadn't even fully unzipped my tent before someone (or should I say something) was giving me a hard time, not trying to conceal her disapproval in the least.

It was Red Fran.

RF: "Tish, what the fuck? How stupid are you?"

She was fuming.

"Oh my God. How about minding your own business?" I replied, flopping onto my Therm-a-Rest.

"Um, how about not making rash decisions like that and just leaving me here to wonder if you're dead or worse?"

"What's worse than dead?" I asked.

"Maybe rape first, then dead," she clarified, trying to scare some sense into me.

"Okay, well, you can calm down now. I'm here. I'm fine. Everything's fine."

"Well, I don't like being left here all alone while you're off doing God knows what with God knows whom."

"Um, thanks *Mom*, but you can back the fuck off now," I replied. She was bored, and jealous no doubt, stuck inside while I was out and about.

I'd bought her because she was sturdy, sensible, and fit with that rugged side of my identity at a time when I was shrugging off the trappings of my well-to-do upbringing. I'd been thrilled to get a good deal on her too. That was part of the appeal, as well as all those supportive straps to heft around all my stuff.

Red Fran and I had gotten to know one another very well during the NOLS trip, and while I found her to be a bit of a pain in the ass, always on my case for saying or doing the wrong thing, I knew she would always have my back. This was about baggage, not luggage, after all.

getting my thrills in victoria falls

. . .

THAT NIGHT, I met Frank at Campsite, the local Vic Falls bar. After a couple of drinks, we went back to his *mess* (a small hut). I wish I could say he seduced me back with a sexy gesture of some sort, but that didn't seem to be the way it went around here. Instead, all he said was "let's go" as if we'd been married for years and it was a given.

Still, he got no argument from me. As someone more accustomed to being overlooked, this was truly out of the ordinary. And even though I watched these guys flirt with all the lady rafting clients, I didn't care. I liked that I could feel them undressing me with their eyes, almost honored to be sexualized. Even though I knew it was not a 'special circumstance', it felt special to me.

Yes, I felt special in a truly pathetic sort of way.

I should also mention that Black men had always aroused a certain sexual appetite in me. Their smooth, hairless skin, their gorgeous smiles... And was it true what they say?

I was scared, but not enough to crush the desire of finding out for myself.

We rode up to his place in a taxi around midnight. I waited outside the cab while he went in to kick out his sister who had been sleeping there. She stumbled down the walkway into the cab, and when she got there, eyes half shut, she gave me the evilest of glares before getting in and driving off. Yikes. I wondered how many times this had happened before.

I felt bad for his sister, which made me feel terribly uncomfortable. But what was I to do? Culturally speaking, the men here had the upper hand. I was on his turf, blindly following his lead, completely unaware of the circumstances of his life. He led me under the mosquito netting and onto the bed where the sheets were awkwardly warm, leaned to the front of the bed and put a tape in the cassette player. When the music began, I couldn't help but laugh.

"Why are you laughing?" he asked, as he pulled my shirt up.

"I just… it's not the music I was expecting…"

"But it is my favorite song, Tish," he said with his beautiful wide grin, humming along while pulling his own shirt off, showing me his sleek, hard abs while Whitney belted, 'I Will Always Love You.'

I knew they were a good ten years behind the times here but this little interlude helped calm my nerves. When it came to skill and confidence in the sack, I was still a bit of a wallflower. He rolled on top of me and planted his voluptuous lips on mine. His body was strong, his skin soft, his cock hard, and it didn't take long before he was inside me.

My friend, I wish I could recount a hot and dirty experience, but I'm not one to lie. Instead, it was rather painful. Plus, I wasn't exactly given the chance to warm up, if you know what I mean. Even if I had been slippery and wet, I promise you one thing… It is true what they say. Very, very true…

While I was pleased that one sexual fantasy had been realized, the whole experience lacked the affection and eroticism I had envisioned would come with it. This realization came to me the next morning when Frank quickly put me in a cab while his neighbors stared upon me in disgrace.

I didn't regret it one bit, but I knew I wanted it to feel different, to feel good.

> **why take the obvious route**
> **when you can see things anew?**
> **if you wanna up your vibe**
> **let go of the old**
> **and give way to a change of mind**
> **now what's your new view?**

But wait, that's not where I meant to end this story! My goodness, my mind is in the gutter. Before we get too distracted by sex, I wanted to tell you about the whitewater rafting on the Zambezi River.

Now that's how I truly wanted to feel! I fucking loved it!

The day began with a long hike down the gorge to the river. The guides, carrying the rafts over their heads, zipped past with ridiculous speed while the rest of us clients cautiously made our way down the steep slope. By the time we got to the bottom, the rafts were already in the water and the guides were waiting.

I was mesmerized by this narrow-walled gorge as we began our adventure downriver. Rapid after rapid, the adrenaline rush did not leave my side. Despite the many times I was certain we were going to flip, we never did.

One noteworthy aspect of this rafting trip were the guys in kayaks. They were our 'safety boaters,' there to save us should anyone fall out. Doing this from their small kayaks seemed highly unlikely, but when one of the other rafts flipped, I was in instant awe of their skills. Throughout the day I couldn't stop watching them as they gracefully and effortlessly made their way down the river--

"Waaaaah!"

I was startled out of la-la-land by a screaming child, and suddenly became aware that I was in Toronto, standing in MEC.

Damn. Back to reality..

a flash of inspiration

. . .

I LOOKED at the River Run brochure in my hand and a deep, automatic inhale washed over me. I felt inspired. Maybe I didn't have to go back to the Zambezi to become a raft guide. Maybe I could do it here?

> listen to your heart
> it knows the way
> let it speak to your mind
> so you know what direction to take

And then it dawned on me how I recognized the River Run logo. While at uni, I had met a guy at a party one night. He had caught my attention because he stood out from the crowd in his raspberry pink fleece. I saw a yellow River Run logo embroidered on it, and when I asked him what it was, he told me he was a raft guide in the summer on the Ottawa River.

How this information all of a sudden came to me was a mystery. But there it was, a distant memory resurfacing to the forefront of my mind. I looked up from the brochure and let out a sigh of relief.

"River Run! I'm going to be a raft guide!"

The idea of it felt so good, and I carried that feeling with me all the way home. Unfortunately, I made the most rudimentary of mistakes as soon as I got there...

I told my parents.

"Tish, that's not exactly what your mother meant when she said to look at the bulletin board at MEC."

Here we go again...

"Really? Then tell me, what exactly did she mean?"

"She was hoping you'd find a real job."

"*She* was hoping or *you* were hoping?"

"Does it matter?"

"It matters that you don't put words in her mouth," I retorted.

"Tish, don't you think you should..."

But there was no way I was going to let my dad finish that sentence. Any time a parent or authority figure began a sentence with "don't you think you should..." my Scorpio stinger was ready to attack. I never have and never will appreciate anyone trying to tell me what I *should* be doing.

"Hey! Don't you think you *should* mind your own business?" I quipped. And I turned around and stormed off before we could get any deeper into this shit pit. At the top of the stairs, I paused to hear my dad raise his voice to my mom.

"Maureen, why would you tell her to go to MEC? Dumbest idea you ever had..."

Back in my room, I was both enraged with my parents and amped about my plan. I wanted to call River Run immediately but forced myself to take a few minutes to calm down. *Just breathe Tish, just breathe.* It helped ever so slightly. *Why does he have to be such a dick?* I thought to myself.

I didn't get it. On the one hand, my parents were these open-minded people who had encouraged me to get out in the world. Yet on the other hand, they completely discouraged me from pursuing a life outside the norm. How could they be so contradictory? In truth, all it did was motivate me to get further away from them where I could freely forge my own path without them trying to pull me back. I didn't want to be 'normal.' I hated the idea of normal!

Finally, I picked up the phone and called the rafting company.

"Hello, River Run Rafting, how may I help you?"

"Hi. Um, this is Tish, um, I want to be a raft guide and I was wondering if you're hiring?"

"I see. Well, we already had our guide training in May, and the season is already well underway, but, um, our guide manager just happens to be in the office, which he never is, so let me see if he's available to talk to you. One moment please…"

"Hello, this is Leo."

"Hi. Um. I'm Tish. I just found out you already had guide training. I know we're in mid-June now, but I'm interested in becoming a raft guide. Is it too late?"

Please God, don't let it be too late. I knew in my heart this was my only option.

"Do you have any experience?" he asked.

"Well, only if you include rafting the Zambezi."

"You rafted the Zambezi? Ace!"

"Well, I was just a guest, but yes."

"Why don't you come on up this weekend, hop in a raft and see how it goes?"

"Oh my God, really? That'd be incredible."

I really had no idea what it meant to be a raft guide, but even so, I could feel I was in the flow.

Thank God.

> **look up at the sky**
> **give thanks**
> **and know**
> **ALL is divine.**

Now I knew I was going away this weekend, I could relax.

The next morning after my dad left for work, I told my mom. It was usually easier to talk to her because she was a kind, supportive person. Plus, she had to play that role to balance out the harshness of my father. I felt for her, having to be the pillar of the family. How can you be yourself when you're busy smoothing out all the rough edges around you?

While I didn't know what she'd expected me to find on the bulletin board of an outdoor adventure gear company, as our conversation unfolded, I realized that driving four and a half hours to become a raft guide was not what she'd had in mind…

"First Africa and now this?"

Ugh. You used to be so encouraging.

"I just… I can't help but worry about you, Tish. I want you to be safe."

"Mom, I'm good! Stop worrying! Someday maybe I'll get an office job and live down the street and have lots of babies so you can relax and be happy."

I was being sarcastic, though by the glimmer of hope in her eyes, I think she took me seriously. But that was never my intention. And the moment I entered River Run and was directed towards the raft guide accommodation, my true intention was only strengthened. I had found my 'real' world. And my tribe.

other weirdos like me

. . .

I DROVE my dark green Dodge Neon into Guide City, a circular field lined with rustic cabins as well as two old, yellow, permanently parked school buses. I stopped next to one of the cabins where some people were hanging out on its small deck. Feeling like the shy kid starting school in the middle of the semester, wandering around the halls looking for my class, I hoped desperately someone would be friendly enough to save me. It's not easy going out on a limb like this!

"Here we go," I steeled myself before opening my door and stepping out.

"Hi there!" a guy in a checkered shirt yelled out to me, beer in one hand, cigarette in the other. "If you're looking for guest camping, it's over there!" and he pointed to another field off in the distance.

"Oh. Um, no, I'm...I'm here to join you guys this weekend, I think? I spoke to Leo and he invited me up?"

"Ohhh right. You must be... Sorry, what was your name?"

"Tish," I said smiling awkwardly at this good-looking outdoorsy guy.

"I'm Duke. Yeah, Leo mentioned you. Well, why don't ya come on up and grab yerself a beer?"

I hopped up onto the deck, painfully aware of more than a handful of eyes staring me up and down. Duke cracked open a Labatt 50 and handed it to me.

"Thanks!" I took a sip and grimaced.

"Ha! Yeah sorry, it's all warm beer here, eh," Duke said, laughing with the others.

At first, I was embarrassed, but as I quickly assessed the faces in front of me, I didn't get the sense they were laughing *at* me. Rather, it was more that they understood exactly what it was like to drink warm beer because they were all doing it as well. It took no time to relax into the casual atmosphere, relieved to be free from the pressures of my parents who always wanted me to look more presentable than I was willing to be. I abhorred anything 'fancy' and resented having to pretend to be anything but myself. And it seemed like these guides were on par with that same sentiment; that they too were non-conformists, the ones who rejected the nine-to-five rat race, the ones mainstream society deemed as weirdos... Weirdos like me.

While I knew the city life clearly wasn't for me, it was still yet to be determined whether or not the 'valley life' was. I had gone from one extreme to the other; paved roads to dirt roads, cityscapes to cow fields, high society to country bumpkin. And even though I fit right in with my Chaco sandals, jean shorts, and Zambezi bungee jumping t-shirt, this new environment was still something of an adjustment.

But why would it be? When I was traveling, the 'dirt life' was no biggie. This was on a par with that. Maybe it was because traveling is a temporary lifestyle, while this, for some reason, I was considering as more permanent. Like, here I am, this is my life now.

Only time would tell.

walk into your day
with kindness and love

**let these two emotions guide your way
and I promise you'll never feel lost
or find yourself astray**

"Hey Tish, I'm Lydia! You can stay in that bus with me if you like," someone said, pointing to the old ratty school bus across the field. "There's an extra bed."

"Okay, thanks!"

Cool, another chick. When I took note of all the guides I had seen so far, we were the only women. Maybe that's why Leo didn't hesitate to invite me up. She was smaller than me, which gave me a little bit of confidence simply for the fact that if she could do this, so could I.

Come to think of it, up until this moment, it hadn't even occurred to me to wonder whether or not I was even capable of the job. I had only been in whitewater once in my life, yet here I was ready to become a raft guide? It made no sense, logically speaking.

But it also made complete sense simply because of how good it felt to be here. That was my driving force, and the force was strong.

A couple of friendly beers later, I headed over to the bus with Red Fran.

"Well, this looks like quite the predicament you've gotten yourself into."

"What do you mean? This is awesome."

"We'll see about that tomorrow, after you embarrass yourself all day..."

"Hey man, have you ever thought of giving me a boost of confidence instead of being such a drag?"

"I'm just a realist. You get what you get."

"Maybe I should've gotten the blue backpack... Maybe it had a better personality."

"Well, now you'll never know."

I inflated my Therm-a-Rest on the spare wooden bed frame and snuggled into my purple sleeping bag. I was nervous about what the following day had in store for me, and even more so from Red Fran's straight talk, but I reminded myself that I felt good about where I was at so far.

I should trust that feeling.

a river run fantasy

. . .

WHITEWATER WAS A FANTASTIC TEACHER. And as it turned out, the Ottawa River was a world-class river. The water is cold and the levels high in the spring, with the temperature warming and levels dropping over the course of the summer.

The river is *drop pool*, meaning you have a rapid, then calm water before another rapid which makes it a fantastic adventure for rafting enthusiasts. Why? Because if you flip or people fall out, you have time to recover before the next rapid.

Another plus is that it's a *big water river*, meaning it's wide and deep. For that alone, many would consider it safer than other commercial rafting rivers around the world.

Remember those safety kayakers I was obsessed with on the Zambezi? Well, they have those here too, but they also have what you call *playboaters*. The Ottawa River is a playboating mecca attracting not-quite-surfers who do tricks on standing waves (meaning the wave stays in one place unlike ocean waves that build, break, and eventually dissipate, all the while moving). The playboaters do these tricks in short, stubby kayaks and the same goes for rafting. You can surf in your raft! It's actually the goal at many of the spots during the day as you float downstream.

get ready for your day
jump in and surf those fears away!
why be afraid of anything?
you've got this...
now GO and SLAY!

The clients loved it and so did I. The weekend was top notch, mostly because the guides were so friendly and helpful, even though they were all initially confused as to my lack of experience.

"So you've never guided before?"

"You don't have any gear?"

"Do you know anything about whitewater?"

These were just some of the questions I got as I sat in the back of a raft, alternating guides. I couldn't argue with their confusion. Why would Leo invite a completely inexperienced person to join them as a potential guide? Essentially, I was a client getting to raft for free. I was a legit poser!

Nonetheless, they were accepting and kind, and maybe it was just because it was so easy for me to fit in and have fun with them that they didn't mind, although it was most likely because my presence increased the girl-to-guy ratio.

On my way home that first Sunday, I stopped at an outdoor store and purchased my own life jacket and helmet so at least I looked like a raft guide instead of a 'punter.' Plus, I desperately wanted to fit in. This was an easy first step.

———

For the rest of the summer, the Ottawa Valley was my weekend destination. I wasn't able to live there full time because I wasn't a qualified raft guide and working as one wasn't an option. Plus, I needed to make money.

Unfortunately, it also meant I had to swallow my pride and

live with my parents during the week. I avoided my dad as much as possible because, in his opinion, this rafting thing was yet another one of his daughter's poor life choices. But I did get work at an office via a temp agency, filling in for someone who was on maternity leave. It was just your basic office assistant boringness, but I managed to pull it off with a smile because it kept me out of the house, and I made some money at a normal job. The parents liked that, obviously.

Most importantly, though, I could make the four and a half-hour drive from the city to the country on a Friday afternoon, returning to the city on Sunday evening. The long drive in traffic didn't even bother me. On the way there, I was full of excitement and anticipation; on the way back, I was on a high, reflecting on the fun of it all.

My circumstances at River Run were special in that I lived in Guide City with the guides while I was there, essentially acting as if I was one, even though I wasn't. Each Saturday and Sunday, I would hop in one of the rafts with a guide and his clients, and go down the river with them. The guide would show me a few things, teach me about the river, and even have me guide some of the easy sections.

In the evenings, we hung out in Guide City, listening to music, drinking beer, and smoking weed. Cigarettes were also a common theme among guides, but I was a terrible smoker and didn't want to spend my money on it, so that habit was short-lived. Sometimes there would be a band playing on Saturday night and we'd go hang out with the guests in the outdoor pavilion or play some beach volleyball.

I loved to walk the 'teehee' trail, a narrow trail in the forest that took us from the pavilion back up to Guide City. But there were rules: you had to be high and you weren't allowed headlamps or flashlights. The path was covered in roots, twigs, and branches, so to walk it in the dark while high, there could only be one reaction:

"Teehee! Teehee!"

Bursts of laughter pealed the entire way as drunk and stoned guides tripped up the hill in the late, dark night. It was one of my favorite things to do.

Then there was Jerry, the video kayaker.

some kind of wonderful

. . .

JERRY'S JOB was to document the day. He'd paddle the river in his kayak, staying ahead of the trip so he could get out to film the rafts from the shore as they went through each rapid. He'd also film when we went cliff-jumping, ate lunch, etc… capturing it all. Then he'd race back to base, edit the footage, and add music to make a 'trip video'.

Once the rest of us were done on the river, we'd gather the clients around the pavilion to watch the video, hand out silly awards, sell some videos, then say our goodbyes. By 4 p.m., our day was complete.

Jerry intrigued me. He was older, cultured, and mysterious (or maybe just moody). He was nice to me and we became friends while I crushed on him silently. Eventually, and I don't know how, I began sleeping in his cabin with him… platonically, of course.

I didn't know what to do or how to make a move. Growing up, I wasn't into looking or acting attractive to guys, so they weren't drawn to me the way they were drawn to my pretty friends. Now I would automatically assume they were not into me *that* way, but apparently that's not true. In fact, Lydia practically slapped me when this other guy Johnny came to the bus to ask if I wanted to watch the Northern Lights and I turned him away because I was too tired.

"Tish, are you kidding?! He's totally into you! And so is Stan! How are you not getting this?"

"What? That's crazy!"

I had no idea their intentions were anything other than what they were *literally* inviting me to do. It was only now, as the summer progressed, that I was beginning to learn that I, Tish, as my true rugged self, actually held sex appeal in the eyes of these guys.

So, when Jerry finally made a move on me in bed one night, it came as a shock and I totally fucked it up!

We were spooning when he said, "Tish, I can feel your leg rubbing up on my--"

Before he had a chance to finish his sentence, I panicked. "Oh my God, I'm so sorry," I said, not catching his tone and swiftly moving my leg.

It was totally reactionary. I was such an idiot. Thankfully, he tried again.

"It's okay. I quite liked it."

And then kissed me.

Oh. My. God. Is this really happening?

We started making out, and wow… I love French kissing! I love the intertwining of tongues. When two people are in sync, it's so hot! I was into it, like, so much. But then, his hands ventured towards my panties and I blurted out "not too much!"

Cringe.

He recoiled and I knew right away that was that. Friendzone it was.

Ugh.

How was I fine cuddling with him in my panties but nothing beyond that? How could I spend so much time dreaming of him, imagining myself with him, wanting more, but freak out when the opportunity presented itself? I was pissed at myself. *What's wrong with me?*

Maybe that's what happened when you grow up at an all-girls private school, go to an all-girls private camp, and at 23 years old have only had sex three times in the last five years!

Thinking I must be as vanilla as they come, I decided I didn't want to be.

desperately seeking somewhere (other than here) for winter

· · ·

TWO THINGS WERE CERTAIN. One, the 1996 rafting season was complete, and two, I was a thousand percent in for 1997. This meant I was committed to guide training for May of the following year, after which I would become a legit full-time whitewater raft guide. *Yes!*

But what was I going to do in the meantime?

I was not alone in this dilemma, which was common for us seasonal river rats. And with the knowledge I would only be making $60 per day guiding trips, the real challenge was how I was going to make enough money in the winter *so that* I could work on the river all summer. You see, from what I had witnessed, most of these river guides were living off of PB&J and ramen. I didn't want that to be me. Money gave me options and a level of independence I was committed to having.

While living with my parents was an option, as well as a good way to save money, it would also be bad for my mental health. Come to think of it, it was probably bad for their mental health as well, not to mention it was imperative I avoid the long harsh winter of Toronto.

I couldn't take anymore of my mom's sly attempts at influencing me, opposite of my father's approach of just blurting out things like, "That makes no sense to me" or "that's the dumbest idea I've ever heard in my life..." My mom was more about unconscious manipulation: "Why don't you try..." or "Wouldn't be a good idea if..." or "Have you ever thought about..." All this was under the pretense of trying to be helpful, but it was trickery, really... It was all based on *her* needs, *her* fears, *her* desires, *her* beliefs... her own hidden agenda.

When it comes to parents, here's what I've learned so far...

We're trained from birth to please and appease them, so we're 'good' when we do what we're told and 'bad' when we go rogue. Over time, we become disengaged from our own inner guidance system so what was once a thunderously loud and clear voice becomes a faint, shy whisper blowing past us in the night.

And so we live under our parents' rules and power until eventually we want to break free from it. Oh yes, this is the juicy bit because now we're ready to turn back to that inner guidance system so we can make decisions on our own. At first, it's scary and disorienting and hard to trust because we've lost touch with that inner guidance. But in time, and if you work at it, your connection with this long-lost friend will become so familiar – like picking up right where you left off.

let nothing come between you and me
for we are the vision of one reality

Once that happens, it's easier to turn within and ask yourself: *What should I do?* Then listen for the answer and do what you need to do for you. When you do, wow! You'll feel empowered, like I did every weekend on the river, listening to my inner guidance that was spot on.

It was a powerful feeling.

And it was time to do that again.

As Jerry and I continued to spend time together, I learned about his postseason plans. In two weeks' time, he would leave for Nepal to work as a video kayaker for a rafting company.

Another buddy, Dave, was heading to Taiwan to teach English for the winter. He and one of the other guides who had been teaching there for a couple of winters said it was really easy to find work and the pay was excellent. You didn't even need to know how to teach. You just needed to speak English!

It was the perfect solution and a no-brainer decision for my adventurous spirit. Excited to solidify my plans, I called a travel agent the very next day and booked my ticket. I would be leaving in six days!

> **enter the zone**
> **just listen to what's true**
> **then relax and let go!**
> **you know you're on the right path**
> **when there's no force, only flow!**

I had a lot to do in a short amount of time. I gathered as much logistical info from Dave as I could, like what hostel to book and how to find work, then I came home to Toronto to unpack, repack, and tell my parents of my next destination. With ticket in hand and only two days before my departure, they knew there was no point in trying to dissuade me, though I could tell by the way my mom was scrunching her face that worry was once again setting in. With my dad, well, he bit his tongue, rolled his eyes, and shook his head.

I was almost impressed. Was it possible they were beginning to let me be or was I just getting smarter at not giving them an opportunity to talk me out of it?

ni hau whaaa?

. . .

September 1996

AFTER 22 HOURS and one overnight layover in Singapore, Red Fran and I landed in the city of Taipei, Taiwan's capital.

"I'm so glad we're on a new adventure. I was getting pretty sick of the bugs and dirt in the valley."

"My God, Red Fran, how are you such a comfort snob? Weren't you made for a rugged life?"

"Um, *excusez-moi*, but weren't *you* made for a comfortable life?"

"Touché, Franny pants, touché."

"Don't call me that."

I knew nothing about Taiwan except for the few things my River Run buddies had shared. One, it was a small island off the coast of China. Two, Taiwanese Mandarin was their official language (which was a different dialect from the Standard Mandarin of China). Three, Michael Jordan was their hero. And four, as a teacher, I would be the token foreigner, which was a necessary element for any school trying to bring in new students.

Going from the lush green valley and the sounds of the river to this concrete jungle was an immediate shock to the system. That's what I love about flying; leaving one runway behind and arriving on another with a whole lot of blank space in between. "See ya, Canada" one moment, "Ni hau, Taiwan" the next. It was culture shock at its very best, and wonderfully invigorating!

It was the same shock as when I landed in Nairobi, even though I had done research and felt prepared for what to expect: the dry orange dust, the overwhelming poverty, and the blasting heat. Yet knowing it and experiencing it are two very different things.

Familiar surroundings give us confidence because we're aware of the habits and patterns around us. That's why being a foreigner is immediately humbling. You get to be in a state of awe, taking it all in like a newborn baby, looking out at the world through wide, curious eyes and where nothing is taken for granted.

In Nairobi, while I was initially dealing with culture shock and scared to leave the hotel that first day, my parched throat combined with the knowledge not to drink the tap water was what eventually inspired the courage I needed to venture outside. I remember buying a Sprite from an old man selling soda and candy out of a decrepit lean-to on the side of the dirt road. I had barely had a chance to quench my thirst before a small, impoverished child in rags snuck up on me from behind, snatched that bottle of Sprite right out of my hand and continued on his way. I had no idea that was something to be aware of!

It was my very first lesson. Next time I would be prepared, I told myself at the time.

> **move freely today**
> **don't let little annoyances get in your way.**
> **just brush them off**
> **let them go**
> **you don't need them anyway!**

Now here in Taipei, I stood just outside the airport exit and had yet to find someone who spoke English. I knew I needed to get a bus into the city center, but which bus? I could stare at these signs all night but, come morning, I would still be clueless as to what those Chinese characters said.

RF: "Alright smarty pants. Now what?"

Me: …

We become so accustomed to having our bearings that it can be unsettling when our eyes don't recognize what's in front of us. The mind doesn't like to feel disoriented! But that's exactly what makes travel so exciting. In the disorientation, you seek clarity, naturally expanding your comfort zone. Yet in the moment, it was an intimidating realization that took culture shock to a whole new level. It was unlike any of the countries I'd visited in Europe and Africa where I could use my broken high-school French to make sense of the signs or find someone who spoke English to direct me if that didn't work. Here, I felt utterly helpless.

Unsure of what to do, I prayed for help. Not in a religious way, just with a simple yet articulate thought that went something like: *Fuck, man, I need a lil' guidance here…*

> **watch and stare**
> **be still and let go**
> **it's okay not to know**
> **just breathe in and breathe out**
> **to feel for the flow**
> **that's how you'll know.**

Not two minutes later, a nice man in a suit approached me. In a reasonable attempt at English, he asked if I needed help.

"Oh, ah, hello? You, ah, like direction?"

He was very shy, looking down as he spoke, almost bowing to me. I would come to learn that the people in Taipei were all about saving face, so approaching a stranger to give help when they may not have the answer happened infrequently. If they didn't know an answer, saving face can look like lying! It may be a white lie, but misleading nonetheless.

"Yes! Thank you! Um. Taipei?"

I would also learn quickly to use basic words and avoid full sentences.

"Oh oh oh, Taipei. Okay okay. Taipei. Where?"

I pulled out my piece of paper where Jerry had written the address of the hostel. I showed it to the gentleman.

"Oh oh, okay. Ah, one moment, ah-please."

And he pulled out a small, handheld electronic thing with a mini-keyboard and began typing in the address. It must have been some sort of translator device. After a minute or two, he responded, "Okay okay!"

He took out a pen from his jacket and began writing in Chinese characters on my piece of paper.

"Now, this-ah bus," he said, pointing to the second bus in the row. "Then, taxi. Give taxi, ah..." and handed me the paper. "Yes. No ah-prob-ah-lem!"

"Oh thank you, thank you!" I said, gratitude billowing out from my tired eyes.

"Yes, no ah-prob-ah-lem!" and off he went to another bus.

After the hour-long ride, the bus pulled in at the main station in Taipei. It was early evening, the sky dark, but the night bright from flashing neon signs on buildings and billboards. It was a smaller, tackier version of Times Square. I felt like I had finally arrived.

I found a taxi with ease and handed the driver the piece of paper from that lovely businessman with the address written in Chinese. And I was ever so relieved when he looked at it approvingly, nodding his head and saying, "Chungshan Beilou."

The roads were packed with hundreds of mopeds, but they seemed of little concern to the driver as he aggressively switched lanes, stepping on the gas one second only to slam on the brakes the next, narrowly avoiding death. It wasn't just one or two people on a moped either. No, it was families of five! Dad driving, Mom at the back, a small child sitting in front of the parents, and two young ones in between. And nobody was wearing a helmet! I sat on the edge of my seat, scared awake, adrenaline coursing through my veins, wanting to watch what was going on, yet also wanting to look the other way. It was terrifying!

My first lesson in Taipei? Clearly, they don't value human life the way I did. Be careful.

Some 15 harrowing minutes later, we turned down a dark alley. This couldn't be right. Are you kidding me? How could this be a hostel? I didn't see a sign anywhere. The driver took Red Fran out of the trunk and I could see she was far from pleased. He pointed to a narrow building in front of us wedged between other equally skinny old buildings, all about five stories high. I flipped nervously through the New Taiwanese dollars I had exchanged at the airport with my traveler's checks and handed him some money. I wasn't sure I gave him the correct amount but he received the bills, got back into his taxi and said, "*Zaijian*" (good-bye), before driving off.

Uneasy, I moved forward up the dark, dirty staircase and stopped at the third floor.

RF: "There's supposed to be a hostel behind that door?"

Me: …

Again, with no sign or signs of foreigners, it seemed highly unlikely. I stood there, waiting, though for what I didn't know. All I knew was that I had nowhere else to go. Besides, what choice did I have except to trust I was in the right place?

> **take a few seconds to breathe**
> **relax**
> **feel your entire life with ease**
> **fly high in your mind**
> **spread your wings**
> **'now' is always the best time**

Me: "Wait, I think I hear someone speaking English."

It was faint, but on the other side of that door I could hear voices…yes, definitely English-speaking voices.

RF: "I hope to God you're right. I'm exhausted."

Me: "Me too."

I took a breath and opened the door. *Here goes...*

the disgraced peanut
butter thief

. . .

LIN TAI TAI, the hostel owner, happened to be there when I walked in, which I later found out was unusual. Apparently, I needed to reserve a bed ahead of time (thanks for nothing, Dave), and was damn fortunate she happened to have one more space. I can't tell you how appreciative I was not to get kicked to the curb my first night there with all my stuff and nowhere to go.

The hostel was a single flat made up of four dorm-style rooms, about 20 beds in total, with two bathrooms. As far as I could tell, all the residents were English teachers. Brits, Aussies, Germans, French… it didn't matter where you came from as long as you could speak English, even if English was your second language.

I was given a top bunk in a mixed dorm room that I shared with three other people, each bed with its own privacy curtain. With no window in this small 12x14 space, it was, unfortunately, a dark cave of stale air stifled with a putrefying body odor. My roommates Tom, Linda, and Tony seemed fine, though it didn't take long for me to get on Tom's bad side.

I was hungry, but it was late. With the world outside a blur of similar-looking old buildings with Chinese signs I could not read, I was afraid that if I went out in my current state of tiredness and hunger, I'd never find my way back to the third floor of this strange building. I was exhausted from the long trip and couldn't stomach the idea of turning on my brain in an attempt to navigate my way around right now. It just wasn't going to happen.

Against mine (and Fran's) better judgment, I snuck into the small kitchen area and stared longingly at a jar of peanut butter sitting on the shelf across from me. I knew that what I was about to do was wrong, but I was desperate. As quickly as I could, I took a piece of bread and the jar of peanut butter from the shelf, grabbed a knife. I wasn't even finished spreading the PB on my bread before I heard a stern voice from behind me.

"Excuuuse me, are you eating *my* peanut butter?"

Dammit. I was caught red-handed.

I could feel Tom's large, round stature looming over me, breathing down my neck from behind. I turned around to face him, utterly ashamed of my actions.

"I'm so sorry, I…"

"That is *my* peanut butter and *my* bread. You see, you can tell because it has my name written on it."

He picked up the jar from the counter and pointed to his name in black ink written across the Jif label.

"I, just, was so hungry, and didn't want to go out…"

"I see," he said, staring down at me disapprovingly with eyes that were bulging through his coke-bottle glasses.

His pale chubby cheeks were turning bright pink, and his short, curly red hair seemed to be standing on end. I feared he would spontaneously combust.

"You could have just asked," he said crossly, and put the jar back in its place on his shelf.

I felt like a little child being scolded by an elder.

"But just so you know, we each have our *own* space for our stuff. You *see*…" he said while pointing to his section of a shelf and then some others, all with names written on masking tape in black marker.

I was not one to lie, cheat, or steal, so the fact that I had a) stolen and b) been caught was mortifying.

"I'm so so sorry. I'm going to get food tomorrow, I promise."

And in complete embarrassment, I squeezed past him in the kitchen doorway and slithered back to our room where I hunkered down in my bunk to eat my forbidden sandwich behind the closed curtain.

RF: "I see that went well…"

Me: "Shut up."

> **find space in your heart**
> **even when you feel dark**
> **let love be your light**
> **now relax - in time you will again shine bright!**

It was a turbulent entrance, and a far cry from the ease and joy I felt upon my first arrival in the Ottawa Valley. Even though I was fully committed to my decision to be here, I suspected it wasn't going to be as easy. Still, if all the teachers here could do it, I could too.

Such was my resolve.

taipei survival tips for avoiding certain death

. . .

FOR SEVEN LONG MONTHS, I worked the grind as an English teacher in various *bushi bans* (private English schools) in and around Taipei. But only barely.

In fact, the only thing that kept me from abandoning my post was the growing stack of cash hidden in my bunk that I looked forward to counting every night like a greedy old miser. Well, that, and because the only alternative would be to move back in with my parents and find a temp job in Toronto in the middle of winter... and that was an even worse option. Trading one kind of misery for another seemed pointless.

The learning curve was steep here. Taiwan is a small, isolated island with little contact to the western world. Consequently, their English is atrocious. Seriously, all you had to do is check out any one of the thousands of mopeds you saw each day and you'd enjoy reading oddly worded slogans like: 'Scooter, the man boy' or 'So Easy, the scooter is all my life' or 'Duke, the modern scooter citizen' or 'CT, for your nice scene.'

Somehow, English wasn't taught in elementary school even though it was one of the test subjects on the college entrance exam. Parents—who needed their kids to score high—were desperate to get them proficient early on so that it wasn't an added strain to their already overloaded junior and high school curriculum.

In response, a few private schools opened up. After seeing them as the cash cows they were, it didn't take long before parents, teachers, and others began to emulate them. Anyone could start a school, and there was no standard curriculum. It was a cultural phenomenon. By the time I arrived, bushi bans were like 7-Elevens—one on every corner.

My days were filled with death-defying commutes to different jobs around the city on my moped 'Cabin, with fashionable feeling,' and I thanked God every night for getting home alive. The Taiwanese seemed to have a blatant disregard for the rules of traffic. Or perhaps weren't taught any. Whatever the case, driving in the city was akin to being in the middle of a battlefield. You must be on high-alert at all times, ready to react either offensively or defensively depending on the situation. I was an aggressive driver, always trying to be ahead of the pack of scooters while waiting for a light to turn green, like a bunch of marathoners at the beginning of a race. It was terrifying at first, of course, but once I became familiar with the lay of the land and knew where I was going, I could take my scooter skills to the next level. A part of me enjoyed the adrenaline rush as well.

Once, I got into a fight with a taxi driver who started turning right from the left-hand lane and almost killed me. This was just one of many instances throughout that particular day, so by that point late in the evening and on my way home after a long day of driving to various teaching gigs, I slammed my fist on the trunk of his car in sheer frustration.

The traffic light then turned red, which was unfortunate, because they lasted fucking forever. The rest of the event happened in slow motion:

The taxi driver opened his door. Out came one flip-flopped foot, then the other.

Fuck. Fuck fuck fuck. This is not good.

Frantically, I looked for an escape, but there was a bus directly behind me, and cars and scooters lined up on either side with not an inch to maneuver. I was completely trapped.

Casually, the driver got out of his car, cool and calm as a mobster about to take out his hit. All I could do was sit on my seat and watch helplessly as he spat betel nut juice (think tobacco chew, except reddish-pink and more common in East Asia) onto the pavement next to his foot, then stomped out his cigarette before walking towards me.

He began yelling.

I flipped up the visor of my helmet in the hopes that he'd notice I was a female foreigner and hence go easy on me. But no, he just tore into me angrily in Chinese. After a solid 15 seconds of this, he completed his rant by punching me in the head and breaking my visor before walking back to his cab. We sat there for another minute or two, and all I could think was how lucky I was that he didn't take my moped keys and throw them into traffic.

The light turned green at long long last and off I went, wedged in the middle of traffic, my hands shaking all the way back to the hostel.

While that might have been the scariest incident, it was not the only one I would experience. Another time I was driving my beloved scooter fairly close to the curb on my way up to Beitou, a town north of Taipei, when a car tried to pass me. He edged me out by hitting my back wheel which pushed me into the curb. I wiped out, my body landing on the sidewalk. He pulled over and stopped in front of me, and I was thinking how nice it was that he was checking to make sure I was okay. But I was wrong. Instead, he walked around to check out his car, looked over to me, splayed out on the sidewalk, yelled at me, then got back in and drove off.

When I say they don't seem to value life, it comes from personal experience. And so, I came up with a few survival tips to get me through life in Taipei that winter.

1. When on foot and crossing the street at an intersection, *never* make eye contact with a driver, despite how

counterintuitive this may be. If they see that you see them, they will drive right in front of you and *you* have to stop if you don't want to get run over. By avoiding eye contact, you pretend you don't see them and hope they wait.

2. If you take the bus, be sure to look both ways before getting off of the bus or else you'll likely get swiped by a moped rushing between bus and curb.

3. Go across the street from the hostel to the five-star Prince Hotel. They have a really beautiful restroom in the lobby. This was where I would go to poop in peace. Sneak into the elevator and up to the rooftop of the Prince Hotel to swim a few laps in the outdoor pool.

4. When hanging out in the lobby of a hotel for some quiet time and air conditioning, know that the gorgeous Black men in suits on business from somewhere in Africa who invite you to their room later for a drink believe you to be a hooker. Yeah. How would I know that? Having just returned from their native land, I was excited to engage with them and just thought they were being friendly. We were both foreigners here, after all. But when I came back to meet them later for our date, they never turned up. And when I went back to the hostel, my friend Karen smacked me on the face and woke me up to the fact that they thought I was lingering in the lobby as a hooker. It must have been a miracle they didn't show. Another time I met a local Taiwanese man in a suit at the mall who asked me to teach him conversational English. I was hustling for all the work I could get and this would be easy peasy, so I was all for it. When we met up a few days later, he seemed disappointed that I was actually trying to teach him English! And even more disappointed when I actually made him pay up for the hour lesson! 500NT was about $45 and I was not here to give my time away. Honestly, I have no idea

why these men got such an impression. I certainly was not giving off that vibe. I didn't even know how! Nor was I dressed to impress. I was chubby, constipated, insecure, and as always, dressed in baggy, unflattering clothes. It seemed ridiculous that anyone could ever think I was soliciting sex.

5. Don't eat street vendor food, even if you find the skewered chicken hearts or rice soaked in pig's blood tempting. The flies are rampant. Oh, and a lot of the meat is actually dog, though nobody would ever admit it.

6. Get out of the city whenever possible where nature can be found in abundance.

Apart from these few tips, I had to adopt the attitude of fake it til you make it, just like all the other token foreigners at the private English schools.

My first job was from 8-11 a.m. at an elementary bushi ban. I don't particularly enjoy the company of small children under age five due to their chaotic puppy energy, so this was my least favorite job. I found it extremely draining, what with all that fake enthusiasm and singing of stupid songs and the repetitive nature of "good morning, class, how are you?" to which they would all reply in unison, like robots.

I had no idea what I was doing and simply made it up as I went along. The Taiwanese teachers would literally throw you into a room and say 'teach.' I wouldn't say I was a great teacher, but I did work at getting better.

A couple of those classes were brand new, meaning it was the first ever English class for these tiny humans. Therefore, I had the interesting task of assigning them their English names—names they would likely keep for the rest of their lives. It was always a fun creative project for me. In one class, I named the students after the *Peanuts* characters.

The kids were always sick with green snot running out of their noses at all times and their baby teeth already black. The poor environment with lack of clean air was not conducive to good health. Yet how could there be clean air when there was no nature? It was virtually impossible to find an actual park with grass.

One day, I happened upon a tiny courtyard with a few small bushes as I walked around Beitou. Out of desperation, I snuck in and sat down on the ground, nestling under one of the bushes to write in my journal. Within one minute, I became nauseated by a horrid aroma. I looked around and, disgusted, I saw that it was littered with doggy doo doo, both fresh and old. I bolted out of there, retching.

It was so depressing.

I even gave up jogging by my second month because it felt so horribly counter-productive. It was stressful trying to navigate around people while inhaling all the vehicle fumes. But the absolute last straw was when I *almost* got attacked by a pack of mangy, tooth-baring stray dogs. (The stray dog population is enormous in Taiwan. They are absolutely everywhere, like gangs who own the streets.)

I promise I am not exaggerating when I say Taipei is a concrete jungle. And sadly, the children I taught didn't know any differently. If their bushi ban happened to have a 'playground,' it would be a very small 8x8 section laid with astro turf and, at most, a little plastic jungle gym. I wondered if they had any idea what it was like to breathe clean air or to play in the grass or hug a tree. I felt for them while simultaneously feeling grateful to be born in Canada.

From 1-3 p.m., I taught middle school, then from 4-6 p.m., I taught a class for adults or had a private session with a high school student.

Like I said, teaching wasn't my thing, but I absolutely put effort into my lessons. Yes, I got fired once or twice when my façade wasn't enough, but on the whole, I think the students enjoyed my presence.

On my birthday, my evening class surprised me with a cake. A high school student took me to the night market one evening and made me try candied cherry tomatoes and *chō dough fu* (stinky tofu), which lived up to its name and then some. Once you got past the smell, it tasted pretty good. Another class invited me to the movies where they enjoyed munching on chicken feet like it was popcorn. And after one of my private sessions with a junior student, the mother always had me eat with them—always rice and a whole fried fish that we'd pick the meat from with our chopsticks.

They loved trying to get me to eat the fish's eyeball, saying "is good for brain!" I couldn't do it. It was worse than coagulated goat's blood. For me, that experience had been enough.

In all, teaching was eye-opening, but the most out-of-the-box job I took was yet to come…

getting naked in front of a bunch of old taiwanese men

. . .

THE OPPORTUNITY CAME ABOUT RANDOMLY when I met another English teacher at a party one night who did the job herself and knew they were looking for someone. The conversation piqued my interest. I loved the idea of making some cash without having to actually do anything. I'd never done something like this before, but hey, if all I had to do was sit still and not talk, why the hell not?

And that's how I got the gig as a nude model.

It was a short scooter ride from my hostel and would only be once per week from 7-10 p.m. for $75. The base pay for teaching was $25 per hour, so in my mind this was bonus money.

The entrance to the studio was in the basement of an old, dark building down yet another side alley, and as I descended the short staircase, I was hesitant of my decision. I entered the room cautiously, but was immediately welcomed by a group of friendly old men. I got the sense they were kind and respectful of my being there. I felt I would be safe. Naked, but safe.

The main gentleman, whose name was Li, showed me to the *shoji* screen where I could undress, and pointed to a silk robe hanging from the screen. I noticed there were eight guys, all busy setting up their new canvases and getting their paints ready. I undressed nervously.

Maybe I don't want to do this?

This thought was like an annoying fly that wouldn't leave me alone no matter how much I swatted at it. Not the kind of person to bail last minute, the only way I would be able to emerge from behind the screen was to get aligned with what I was about to do. So I gave myself a moment to focus inward. I took a few quiet breaths and remembered that I had chosen this, that it was okay to be scared and that it didn't need to stop me from moving forward.

I'm in an amazing position
because this is the position I'm in

I came out from behind the screen and Li politely showed me to the small platform in front of the easels and said, 'You go, lay, anything. Yes?'

I stood quietly in my robe, staring at the platform unsure of what pose to strike.

"Ah, maybe like this?" he suggested and he lay down on the platform to give me an idea. "First time, so you do easy. Yes? One hour, you take break."

I smiled politely, nodding in agreement. He got up and went over to his easel. I could feel everyone's eyes on me, eagerly waiting to get started.

Here goes nothing.

I unrobed quickly and lay down on my back. I straightened one leg, the other bent at the knee. I put one hand on my stomach, the other at my side. I stared up at the ceiling and froze. They began.

Never in my life had I imagined doing something like this. Was I comfortable being in the nude in front of a bunch of strange old men? Of course not! I was not even comfortable staring at myself in front of a mirror let alone this. But as the minutes passed, I was slowly able to relax, fall into the silence of the room and even revel in it. It was a welcoming contrast to my exhausting daily routine.

> **let the air you breathe**
> **be your channel for peace**
> **take it in deep**
> **and let your soul speak**

After an hour, I was able to take a break. It actually went by pretty quickly and I wasn't even stiff. I put on the robe and took a moment to stretch before wandering to the front area where there was a large collection of paintings leaned up on the wall. It must have been from other evenings. I noticed some of the red-headed English teacher who got me the gig. Some paintings were better than others, and it was clear these men were artists of varying degrees.

They encouraged me to look at their paintings of me so far. It was not easy to look at their interpretation of my body. Maybe it was more that I didn't like to see how I actually was. In every single painting, I was chubby. Belly, chin, thighs... rolls every-where. It was appalling and I wanted to cry. When I had first arrived in Taiwan, I was hopeful of meeting some fabulous guy, but now looking like this? There was no chance of that happening.

I lay back down for the next two hours and wallowed silently in self-pity. It wasn't easy to eat healthy here. I had no motivation to cook in the dark and grimy kitchen at the hostel, and they didn't have much fresh cuisine to choose from at the cafeteria-type restaurants. I often just snacked on random things like wasabi peas or *dou sha bao*, soft and fluffy steamed buns stuffed with sweet red bean paste filling. It should hardly be surprising that I had gained weight. My pants were definitely not surprised. Yet it was truly horrible to see it mirrored back to me in these paintings.

Nevertheless, I kept this job for a few months. As much as I hated my body, I enjoyed the quiet time more. Each week was a new posture, some harder to maintain than others. During the times my body ached, each minute felt like an hour, but I couldn't do anything except breathe, focus on something else, and know that eventually the time would pass.

One evening during my break, one of the men came up to me and said, "You must take care of body."

I knew right away he was referring to the tiny red spots I had all over my body. Yep. Bed bugs. I had already mentioned the issue to Lin Tai Tai at the hostel, but it was clear she wasn't going to buy new mattresses. Do you know how hard it is to sleep, knowing there are microscopic bugs crawling all over and biting you? That dank room was challenge enough, but towards the end of my trip when I began allowing myself to dream about going home to the Ottawa River, my patience wore thin and I was itching to get out of here. Literally.

After working my ass off for seven months while escaping death on the daily, I knew I had traded my health for wealth and it was time to get back to health. I was so, so ready for a little first-world normalcy. Was it wrong of me to crave the comforts of my old room at my parents' house or to feel safe in my car and go grocery shopping at the fabulous Loblaws or eat my mom's home-cooked meals and lounge around on a comfy couch in our fancy family room? OMG, I couldn't wait to have my own bathroom!

It was easy to glamorize going home with the main focus being on the luxury of comfort, but I had learned from this mistake when I had returned from Africa the previous year. This time I already knew that my enthusiasm for home would be short-lived. It didn't matter though. My transition at my parents' place would be short-lived too.

This time, there was no reason to stress out.

This time, I had a legit plan.

As bleak as this Taiwan adventure sounds, I had no regrets. At least not now, *after* the fact. It taught me that I was willing to be miserable to make a buck and that that's not necessarily something of merit. It taught me that I was willing to jump in head first into a job where I had no experience or knowledge. It taught me that the Taiwanese people (their driving antics aside) are kind, generous, and genuinely interested in being of service.

And it taught me I could do anything I put my mind to.

parents, they just don't understand

· · ·

May 1997

AS ALWAYS, one week at my parents' house was more than enough. Actually, I'm being generous. The first night was good and it was all downhill from there. Why do they insist on trying to rein you back when they know damn well it would backfire? Why can they not help themselves? I just didn't get it.

RF: "What do you expect? They're your parents. Stop trying to get them to get you. They want the opposite of what you want."

Me: "Yeah? What's that?"

RF: "Stability, you idiot."

Me: "Why are you always so mean?"

RF: "I'm not. I just say it like it is. No filter."

Me: "Maybe you're on the spectrum."

RF: "It would be an honor."

Me: …

RF: "By the way, can you give me a wash please? I'm covered in filth and I can't stand it. Thank God we're finally out of that damn stinking hostel! Don't ever do that to me again!"

Me: "Wow. You hated the dirt of the bus, then the stink of the hostel. You're impossible. But yeah, Mom will be thrilled to put you in the wash."

RF: "What? No, hand wash only."

Me: "Jesus, fuck, you're incorrigible."

RF: "Thank you."

Me: …

Throughout the week, whether at dinner, on my way out to meet a friend, or while quietly minding my own business in the morning over a bowl of cereal, the questions were ever-present:

"How could you want to go live up *there* and do *that*? Where is being a raft guide going to take you in the long-run? Do you really want to live your life as a bum? I have a contact at the bank downtown. Do you want me to see if I can get you an interview?"

Jesus, people! I'm sorry I'm such a disappointment to you!

The agony of feeling trapped in these futile conversations that I had no interest in having (for the hundredth time) was demoralizing. As much as I loved my parents and everything they'd done for me, it hurt to know that what I wanted wasn't good, or good *enough*, for them.

Worse, it made me resent them for trying to influence me. I wished their words could just roll off my back. Every time I came home, that was my intention. So far, it wasn't working, and it sucked to know that what made me happy made them unhappy. Still, they would not dissuade me from my path, and I was at least glad that my inner drive towards what felt good for me was stronger than the pull towards doing what felt good for them.

This was *my* life, and these comforts of home were hardly worth the disturbance to my peace of mind. By day seven, I 'peaced out' of there as fast as I could, hoping I would not have to learn this lesson again. It was all very dramatic.

In my privileged little world as an upper-class white Canadian, it only made sense that my detour from conformity would cause chaos. I guess you could even go so far as to say this was my version of a rite of passage. And even though it was not easy to go my own way (though for sure far less painful than getting circumcised), I could feel in my heart that it would be harder to conform. In the long run, it would be soul-crushing, and to me that might be worse than death.

As I made the familiar four-and-a-half-hour drive to the valley, I remembered wondering last year how anyone could live at River Run full time. All that was provided for us in the field of Guide City was... well, not much. A very basic shared kitchen, an old outhouse, the cabins and two buses. The nearest town of Beachburg, five km away, had one small grocery store, a post office, a bank, and a greasy pizza joint. If you blinked while driving through its main street, you'd miss it. But after the chaos of Taipei, I was no longer afraid and, in fact, welcomed the simplicity of small town life.

I was one of the first to arrive at River Run, and eagerly staked my claim in one of the small cabins. It was a glamorous upgrade from the bus, a space all of my own, and a place to call home.

Me: "Is this to your liking, my queen?"

RF: "By your standards, this is luxury. So, yes, I will agree it is acceptable. Just keep the mosquitos out, will you?"

Me: "That's a good sport."

RF: "Hey, is Jerry coming back?"

Me: "I'm not sure. I don't think so."

I found out from Leo later that day that Jerry was still in Nepal. It seemed he was skipping the season here. I didn't mind, actually. I felt so repulsive that I wasn't keen on him seeing me like this. As the other guides started to arrive, my insecurities about myself and my body began to fall away. There were other things to focus on, like what was ahead of us for the next two weeks of training.

It was a summer of bliss... and firsts. My first time guiding a group of guests down the river, my first time kayaking whitewater, and best of all my first orgasm.

dusty and coliseum

. . .

HIS NAME WAS DUSTY.

Our guide manager Leo hired him after watching him playfully and crazily bomb down Coliseum, the biggest rapid of the river. He would be a safety kayaker as well as a raft guide.

It was the beginning of May—spring—which meant high river levels. The dam-controlled Ottawa River was having its spring runoff because of all the melting snow. This was the perfect time for guide training because the stakes are higher in these conditions. More water means the river was flowing faster, so you have to work fast if you flip a raft. Recovery before the next rapid is essential, otherwise it's going to be a major shit show. 'Carnage' as we call it.

In spring, the water was super cold, as was the air. Add to that some rain and you got some long, cold, happily exhausting days.

With so much to learn in two weeks, the adrenaline was always pumping. Guiding was a massive team effort, so during the day we learned how to work together in order to get our future guests down the river safely. You had the 'trip leader,' who always went down the rapid first. You had the 'sweep,' who always went last, with the rest of the rafts between. The river was a living breathing being of its own; you had to be on point and quick to react when things didn't go as planned.

In the afternoons and evenings, we drank beer, had campfires, and laughed a lot. Dusty and I became quick friends. He was fun and friendly, easy to be around, and happy to help me work on my kayaking roll down at 'the beach' (the waterfront area of River Run) after work. I was eager to soak up his knowledge of the river and I was stoked he was so patient with me.

The downside was he was a hick. A small-town farm boy from one of the neighboring areas, just like most of the other guides. Think 'Footloose,' but instead of farmers, they've turned into river guides; instead of cowboy boots, Tevas; and instead of cowboy hats, helmets. I found that weird country-boy accent cringeworthy —"I seen him on the river yesterday" or "yer paddle ain't long enough". Oh and get this, the first time we went out for dinner he needed to borrow money.

It was all a major turn-off for this privileged, private-schooled city girl. As cute as he was, I couldn't be attracted to him.

With the training complete and the season underway, all focus was on getting our clients down the river safely. It was a big responsibility and I was nervous to be in charge of 12 people in a massive black rubber raft. Those 12-foot rafts were tanks, and you needed the clients' help getting to where you wanted to be, which meant there was always a lot of yelling on my part: "Back on the left!" (people on the left side of raft needed to paddle back), "Forward on the right!" (people on the right needed to paddle forward), "Easy forward," "hard forward," "all back!!"

And my favorite: "Everybody get down!"

That last one happens when you need everyone to get off their seat and squat before you hit a massive wave because it's going to jostle the raft. If you're not on line (and even if you are), people are likely to get thrown out.

In high water, there are two rapids that need to be double-guided, meaning you need a guide at the front of the raft as well as a guide at the back. That's because both of these rapids have multiple waves you had to hit at varying-but-exact angles in order not to flip. The first rapid—The Lorne—was right before lunch (a barbecue on the river's edge, at the bottom of said rapid). The second one—Coliseum—was closer towards the end of the day.

Half of the rafts would park at the top of the rapid, tie off, and the guides would leave their clients to hop into the rafts of the other half of the group. I always teamed up with Dusty. So I'd jump in his raft and guide from the bow (front) to help him take his clients down, send those clients to lunch and run up the shoreline back to the top of the rapid to take my clients down.

The adrenaline was pumping, especially for Coli, and most of us guides couldn't eat lunch because our nerves made our stomachs churn in anticipation of it. Coli is the biggest rapid on the river in high water, comprised of three massive waves, each of which must be hit with speed so that you can 'punch through' the waves. Without momentum, it's like running into a concrete wall, except the wave will not only bring your raft to a halt, but its own momentum will push your raft backwards and flip.

It was considered a Class V rapid, which was the highest difficulty ranking based on technical difficulty, margin for error, and consequence. As a contrast, Class I is basically flat water or very light current.

The clients had to be clearly briefed at the top of the rapid in terms of what we needed from them. And unlike other rapids where we would tell you to hold on to the raft if you fell out, if you fell out here you were told to abandon ship and swim to the right as hard as you could, which is not easy to do in a wetsuit and lifejacket, with paddle in hand and most likely disoriented. This was a big deal, because with this particular rapid you didn't have much time before the water quickly pushed into another rapid, and you didn't want to swim down that ledge, I promise you that.

Given the difficulty, each rafting company had its own zodiac, a motorized raft, essentially. They would watch as the rafts came down the rapid, and if one flipped, they would zoom out to the bottom of the rapid and start grabbing clients who were desperately trying to swim, yanking them into the zodiac by the shoulders of their life jacket and throwing them into the boat as quickly as possible before grabbing another person. It was not graceful, nor was it meant to be. Imagine trying to chase after swimmers in moving water. Those drivers had a very intense, very sexy job.

Dusty and I had a clean record so far, having paired up every day for the last two weeks. That was 14 river trips, with two rapids to pair up, and two rafts per rapid, for a total of 56 wins. We had a good rhythm going. Symbiosis, you might say.

On this particular day, the water level was a foot higher. That means faster moving water and even bigger waves. I was an extra kind of nervous waiting at the top of Coli as we watched the rafts from Wilderness Tours go down ahead of us. Carnage everywhere. It had to be one raft at a time. The next raft couldn't go until the zodiac was ready, but with so many 'swimmers,' there was a longer delay than usual. By the time it was our turn, my nerves were at an all-time high.

We started at the top of the rapid in our usual position, paddling from the right side of the river towards the left, setting up for our first hit. With the water moving faster at this higher level, we were not properly aligned at the time we needed to be. I was leaning out of the front of the bow sweeping my paddle as hard as I could to adjust our angle, and I could hear Dusty yelling at everyone, "Paddle hard! Hard! HARD!" With my front row seat, I could see we were going to hit this thing practically sideways which meant we were a thousand percent fucked.

Normally, when we'd hit the first wave, I, in the front of the boat, would already be over the peak, and would look back to see the raft in the meat of it. Imagine being at the front of a rollercoaster at the peak of a climb and looking back at the people behind you. Doing this, I'd get a good view of the angle of the raft so that I knew what I had to do next. At that point, I'd swap my paddle to my other hand and start sweeping to the right to get us lined up for the second wave. Once through, I'd once again sweep left and try to straighten us out before hitting the third and final 'mystery wave,' fittingly named because it surges dramatically and you never know where exactly it would pop-up or what it would be like when you hit it. If it's green, that's good. If it's breaking, it means there was a force of water surging against us, which was what stopped the raft if you didn't have enough speed.

Today, it didn't matter. We were toast the second we rammed sideways into the first wave and were immediately picked up by the wave and body-slammed back to where we came from—now upside down.

Now we were all on our own. The guides, no matter what, were to stay with the raft, but I went so deep that I was separated. Eyes wide open, I looked around. It was dark. I was so far down that I hit the bottom. I caught faint flashes of green.

Oh, now I understand why others who have been here before have so aptly named this the green room.

But there were no couches here. Just silence. An eerie, yet calming and terrifying silence. It was the loudest silence I'd ever known.

I had not trained to hold my breath and my lungs were screaming for air. It was hard to tell how long I'd been under, but it felt like it was for sure more than a minute. I wondered if this was it for me. I climbed my way up, only knowing which way was up because I could see a spark of light. Finally, my lifejacket caught some momentum and just when my lungs were about to force me to inhale water, my head broke the surface and I gasped for air.

The ordeal felt like one of those down-to-the-wire movie scenes where the hero stops the bomb at the final second.

I had to get my bearings ASAP, so I looked around and real-ized I had traveled two-thirds of the way down the rapid under-water. Clients were everywhere and even though I was still gasping for air, I started yelling at people to "swim, swim, swim!"

The raft was close by and Dusty was already on top of it. He reached his paddle out for me to grab, and hauled me up. While the zodiac fished our clients out of the water, we paddled our massive rubber raft, upside-down, towards shore. Maneuvering a raft upside-down is like trying to drag a dog on its leash when it's lying down and doesn't want to move. Dead weight. But it was imperative we get it to shore before the next rapid, otherwise it was a nightmare and embarrassing putting our clients in other people's rafts and dropping them off wherever we ended up.

We made it to the eddy in time, counted heads, and were happy to know our 12 people were safe, with just a few bruises and scrapes to the arms and knees from clawing themselves up onto the rocks or from being slammed into the zodiac.

Dusty and I, however, were not done. With no time to rest, we ran up the shore to do it again. Out of breath, we de-briefed as we hiked up along the rocks as fast as we could.

"Okay" (panting)... "we... need to get... our angle... straight out of the gate..."

"Ooooeeee... let's not the fuck this up again, Tish... I don't... got it in me..."

"I know... oh my god... dude... I was in the green room..."

"Daaaammmnnn... how... was... it...?"

"Cold... scary... can't... go there... again..."

"We... got... this... Tish..."

My clients were freaking out after having watched us flip Dusty's raft. I used it to my advantage.

"Hey, we got this. Just be on point with our directions, and don't chicken the fuck out. The only way to do this is by working together. We need power and speed, and you guys are the ones that do that."

Dusty chimed in. "Nobody can get down until we say 'get down'. Got it?"

They nodded their heads, hyper alert. I was glad they were all adults. Small children were useless when it came to actually pulling water with their paddle.

"I said YOU GOT THIS???" Dusty yelled louder.

"WE GOT THIS!!!" they yelled back in unison.

At the same time, we got the go-ahead paddle raise from Leo at the bottom of the rapid. Take two. I pushed the raft off the shore.

> **happy days are full of sweet, fun and sometimes**
> **scary waves**
> **we ride 'em high**
> **and duck 'em low**
> **round and round we go**
> **getting wet**
> **then letting them go**
> **so have a nice day**
> **and remember to play**
> **surprise yourself as much as you can**
> **and in every which way**

"Easy forward!" Dusty yelled as he found the angle we needed to exit the eddy. Our eyes met briefly, syncing our energy. There would be no time for words, and I could feel that this time we had an intuitive advantage. I turned around to face the front of the boat and began sweeping immediately from right to left.

Already I could feel we were in better alignment.

Looking ahead, I could see the 'hockey stick' in the wave coming up. It was the corner in the wave that we were aiming for. That was the ticket through. Without turning around, I gave a quick thumbs-up so that Dusty knew we were on the right path. A few seconds later, at the very last second, I turned around and yelled at the top of my lungs…

"GET DOWN!!!"

It was a sight to behold, that moment captured like a Polaroid.

The crew lifted their paddles out of the water and squatted down, grabbing onto the side rope while Dusty dug his paddle in at the back of the raft, securing our line. I turned back around and dug my paddle in at the front, protecting the line from the front.

It worked. We hit the wave with force and slid across its face like a windshield wiper just like we wanted. This automatically straightened the raft, lining us up to hit the next wave at the precise right angle we needed. *Bam!* I turned around and shouted the next instruction.

"GET UP! PADDLE FORWARD!"

Everyone scrambled to get back on the seats. Dusty was shouting at them again too as I turned back around in anticipation of the mystery wave.

"HARD FORWARD! HARD FORWARD!"

Angles and speed are everything in rafting, and there was still one wave to go. I scanned in front of me, desperately searching for it, when it came up out of nowhere from right underneath us like a whale breaching the water. With no forewarning, we were catapulted into the air where our paddles were of no use. It was only for a brief moment, but it passed like an eternity where everything moves in slow motion. We were at the will of the water and all we could do was wait and see how we landed…

KATHUNK!!!

The raft hit the water first, and then I hit the raft, landing chin first before falling into the front compartment. I scrambled to my feet as fast as I could.

We were upright. Everyone was still in the raft. Dusty was sitting like a statue in the back, his paddle in the water, seemingly unaffected. Our eyes met briefly. He was grinning ear to ear. My momentary panic turned to ease when I saw his calm.

"EVERYONE GET UP!!!" I yelled.

Dusty followed up, "EASY FORWARD, FOLKS, EASY FORWARD!"

"NICE JOB, EVERYONE. WAY TO GO. WE DID IT!"

The crew cheered. We headed towards the rest of the rafts in the eddy, relieved and thrilled.

———

That evening, Dusty came by with a couple of warm beers. We cracked them open and recounted the events of the day, reveling in its epicness. He praised me for the role I played, making me blush. I wasn't used to being appreciated in the way he appreciated me. He had faith in my ability as a raft guide, even though I was completely new. And when I spoke, he listened intently, present to every word I said no matter what it was, and no matter the topic. It was nice to feel heard. And his personality had grown on me. The big annoyances I felt from his poor grammatical skills and lack of funds had slowly faded into the background as his kindness and generosity had made its way to the forefront, his chipped tooth smile now a welcome sight, genuine as it was.

There was no denying his kayaking skills were damn sexy.

The rest of the guides had been joking incessantly for weeks already that we were hooking up, even though we weren't. Night after night in response to some sexual innuendo from one of the other guides, one of us would inevitably have to insist we were just friends. Until tonight.

Tonight, they would be right.

He took things slow, sensing my need for it. I hadn't realized before how guarded I was being, until I felt his touch piercing through it. He tuned in to the moment, honoring where I was, not trying to force anything. I needed that. It was sweet. Innocent. A gentle touch here, a caressing there, kisses everywhere. Sadness came over me, noticing how hard this was for me, this allowing of connection, of touch, of vulnerability. The suit of armor I wore was thick. I wondered how it got there and what it would take for it to go away.

As the aromatic candle in the windowsill slowly burned, flickering softly with the breeze, I surrendered, trusted, hoped, and desired just a little bit more than I had before.

the beatdown

. . .

I HAD MADE up my mind. Today would be the day I would paddle McCoy's without swimming.

McCoy's was the first rapid of the river and it was a biggie. There are a few different 'lines' through it, and I wanted to do the one called 'thread the needle.' Essentially, it means paddling between two giant holes on a diagonal. You had to clip the corner of the first one, then turn your boat at a very specific angle so as to avoid the one below it. It was an intimidating rapid, and therefore an intimidating way to start the day. There were no warm-up rapids, like skiing a few blue runs before hitting the black diamond.

It also set the tone for the rest of the day. Get through it and you build confidence for the next one. Get your ass kicked and it makes you question what in the fuck was the point.

Labor Day—and the end of the season—was fast approaching, and it had been almost four months since the beginning of the season. I had garnered a fair bit of knowledge of whitewater by now, but even with that experience, in a kayak, it was so damn easy to flip over. As a beginner, you spend more time swimming than kayaking!

Kayaking was by far the hardest sport I'd ever tried, with a steep learning curve too. The only way to get over that 'hump' was to practice regularly, like every day for weeks. You had to get your soggy ass up and try, try, try again, even when you feel completely defeated. Plus, the whole process of 'swimming' is exhausting.

First, you enter the rapid desperately hoping you don't catch an edge. But if you're not angled and/or leaning correctly —*whoosh!* —there you go.

Second, try to roll as many times as possible (because you quickly learn that swimming is a pain in the ass) until you run out of air and the fear of drowning leads to a minor underwater panic.

Third, you have to grab the handle of your sprayskirt (the rubber thing around your cockpit that keeps the water out) and pull. Then, you have to push yourself out of your boat.

Fourth, hold onto your paddle because it could disappear downstream and that's a real problem when it comes to getting the rest of the way down the river, not to mention the cost of replacing it.

Fifth, grab your boat (unless someone is there to help you out), which is now full of water, and, with both hands full, do your best to kick yourself and your gear to shore.

Six, drag your ass onto shore, empty your boat, take a moment to catch your breath, get back in and try again.

I had gone through this process multiple times at McCoy's, and I was over it. I had to defeat this menace. Today, as he always was, Dusty was with me, ready to fish me out of the water and/or save my kayak from going downstream.

"Tish, you got this. Ain't nothing gonna get in yer way today."

Just the thought of this rapid made my stomach turn. As we paddled the flatwater section, getting closer and closer to the horizon line, my nerves were at an all time high.

But I was determined.

Dusty paddled ahead of me, and I followed behind him. At least, that was the plan. But somewhere in those eight paddle strokes, I was not where I should have been and exactly where I should not have been.

I was headed straight for Phil's Hole, a hydraulic of water that churns like a massive washing machine. Phil's Hole beatdown was a familiar experience. You hit this wall of water and it stops you like it's hammer time. Then, you slide backwards into its pit of hell, the same kind of feeling you might anticipate with fear of an elevator falling, plunging you to your death. Your kayak, a very buoyant object, is now at its mercy, bouncing around in this hydraulic with you attached. A human rag doll. You lose all sense of spatial awareness as you get throttled. Are you upside-down or right-side up?

So here I was in a violent, embarrassing ritual that nobody could help me escape. At some point, my paddle was torn from my arms, and after holding on for as long as I could with the hope of getting washed out of the rapid, I finally pulled my sprayskirt to get the hell outta Dodge. I had to swim the second part of the rapid, which I was used to by now, eventually making my way to shore, with Dusty picking up my scattered pieces of equipment along the way.

This was not over.

> **go for gold!**
> **throw down and own**
> **ALL that you want**
> **take charge of your dreams**
> **your thoughts and your goals**
> **have fun with your life**
> **and you'll never grow old!**

I took a few moments to gather my dignity before grabbing my paddle from Dusty, throwing my boat on my shoulder, and without saying a word, hiking back up the shoreline to the top of the rapid to run it again. I would do it as many times as it took, God damn it. And now that the nerves had been shaken off from the first beatdown of the day, I was now pissed off enough that my determination trumped the fear.

But once again, a disaster hit.

I was caught in the web of Phil's Hole, getting an even worse beating than the first. This one rattled me so hard that it somehow managed to suck my baseball cap out from underneath my helmet. Lost to the river gods, it would never be seen again.

By now, a few people were standing along the shore being thoroughly entertained by my pain. "Ooh, here she goes for another round!" I heard someone say as I walked past and up to the top of the rapid for my third attempt.

I knew now, from those last two attempts, where I had gone wrong. This time, I will get it right. Dusty, of course, had been telling me to turn my boat upstream and 'ferry' at a two o'clock angle. This, essentially, allows you to traverse across the river without moving downstream. I had not been doing this. It was scary to turn your boat to face upstream! It felt counterintuitive because I would have no clear sight of Phil's, or the rest of the rapid for that matter.

I drifted as close as I could to the first hole—Satler's—and clipped its edge, then quickly corrected my angle so that I was facing upstream and paddled hard, blindly praying that I would miss the pull of Phil's. He was not that charming, after all. I glided across to the eddy on the other side, avoiding Phil by an insanely wide margin.

Turns out it was so fucking easy!

Dusty was in the eddy, prepared for more carnage, I'm sure, but instead he paddled up to me and gave me a high five and a big, proud smile. The people on shore were cheering for me and I felt all sorts of relief. I really did not have it in me to deal with another beatdown, either emotionally or physically.

With the rapid that stressed me out the most now out of the way, I could relax. It was ironic, really, because the best thing to do in whitewater kayaking is to relax, especially in the bigger, more intimidating rapids like the one I just ran. Rivers, as you know, run downstream. They curve and weave around bends. They go under, over, around rocks, trees, or any other obstacle it meets in its path. It never tries to control its flow. It simply lets go.

With that in mind, as a kayaker, it would be best to be like the water you're traveling on, right? Right. And with time, you will be. So much so that you'll barely need to put in a paddle stroke. That's how in sync you'll be with the rapid, even on very large, technical ones.

As a beginner, though, it's not so easy to let go of control, which makes it impossible to feel for the flow. In other words, when you meet the current with tension and rigidity, you're just never going to sync up. Instead, you'll catch an edge and flip over. It's a dance. And the water, with its current, is your partner. It takes the lead; you follow.

Continuing on, I paddled the rest of the river successfully, though I promise none of it was pretty. I caught my edge on numerous occasions but managed not to flip. I was mostly tense. Yet I clung to those fleeting moments of calm and connection.

After the day's triumph, I was ready for more. I didn't want the season to end! In two weeks, Labor Day weekend would be upon us, which meant fall was coming, which also meant winter was coming.

Point being, it would be time for me to pack up and go.

pack light

. . .

DUSTY WAS PLANNING to join me wherever I decided to go. Was it risky traveling with a new boyfriend? Sure. But I was having so much fun finally having him by my side that I wasn't ready to let him go... or the regular sex I'd been having for the first time in my life!

Since Dusty had no money, the only real plausible plan was to go back to Taiwan. I know, I know. What was I thinking going back to a place where I was miserable? That's fair, but this time I had a partner, and I'd always wanted to travel with a boyfriend. Maybe having him there would make Taiwan a better experience.

I had to lend him money for the plane ticket, which was fine because I knew he would be able to pay me back within the first couple of months. What I didn't know was that the dude had never been anywhere before.

"So, er, when should we go to the plane station?" he said, his face serious, nervous even.

I paused. A shared moment of awkward silence.

"Say what?"

Surely, he was joking?

"Well, um..."

Okay maybe not.

"You mean the airport?" I replied calmly, still sussing out the situation.'

"Oh yeah, right, that's what I meant."

His voice softer, I could tell he was embarrassed. Still, he continued.

"So do we, er, just go to the airport, get a ticket and hop on the plane?"

Sweet Jesus, what have I gotten myself into?

"Dude, it's not like the bus station. We have to book our tickets beforehand..."

Shoot. I then realized I may have gotten a little ahead of myself. It honestly hadn't occurred to me that he hadn't been anywhere before. I figured everyone wanted to leave their home-town and explore the world. Apparently, that was not true. Or maybe he did, but didn't have the means...

"Hey, um, Dusty, have you ever been on an airplane?"

"Well, ah, er, only if you count that time I went skydiving..."

"I see. So you've never been outside of Canada?"

"Never been, nope."

"Hmm. Hey, do you happen to have a passport?"

It was most unlikely given the direction of this conversation, but I had to ask.

"As a matter of fact, I do! Got one last year when my grandpa was going to take me, my brothers, and my parents to Europe. But then he died, so that didn't happen."

"Ooooh. Crap. Sorry."

"Nah! Hehe, old man kicked it in his sleep. It's fine, eh."

"Okay, well, um, that's good you've got your passport, though..." I said, cringing as the words came out of my mouth, wondering if I was being insensitive for not wanting to talk about his dead grandfather.

"Yep, got er in my cabin somewhere. Anyways, you wanna go surf Push Button?"

I took his response to mean that he was either clearly fine, or he didn't want to take it any further himself. Either way, I was relieved to move on. We loaded our boats and gear into his beater of a truck, added a few more boats and kayakers, and off we went.

Push Button was a really fun, small wave at the second rapid that we could actually drive to directly. In other words, 'park n play' because you don't have to paddle the whole river for access. It was a great spot to practice my whitewater roll as I was guaranteed to flip over after trying to surf the wave, but also an easy spot to rescue myself without drifting downstream.

Since the sun didn't set until 9 p.m. or so during peak summer, we had spent many an evening here. I cherished those nights, sitting on the little rock island next to the wave, watching Dusty surf, trying to surf myself, hanging out with friends, drinking beer, and smoking a spliff in the muggy heat whilst getting a break from the swarming mosquitoes on shore.

> **sunset surfs are the best**
> **a lovely way for the tired mind to rest.**
> **be free, I say**
> **as the waves wash over me.**

But tonight, as dusk fell upon us in this beautiful valley, I was especially in awe while taking in the sight of it all. Fall. The leaves were starting to change color with hints of red or orange or yellow pigment on the surface. The air was perfectly fresh, the water dropping a few degrees, and the scent of the earth musky-sweet with decaying plants.

Prior to arriving here, I had been searching for my people. But why? What was it I thought I would get by finding them? What feeling had I believed I was missing?

I knew now what that feeling was. Connection.

When trying to come up with words to describe that feeling, they all fall woefully short of the visceral experience I was having. The land, the water, the people. Like we're all part of a familial 'clan'. Like we'd shared this space together before, were torn apart, and somehow found our way back to one another. I imagined it would be like reuniting with a long-lost love.

It hadn't been easy, though! Finding this connection had required me to take charge of my direction and follow my heart. That's what had led me to the entrance of River Run. And when I took into account the influential forces of society trying to get me to conform, having the courage to do as I pleased made the journey that much sweeter.

I felt lighter for it too. Not just in my body thanks to an active summer on the river, but in my mind. I had been carrying the weight of the world on my shoulders, and now that I was beginning to find and accept myself, that weight was beginning to lift. Like a fog that had blurred my vision, I was beginning to see my path. What a relief!

At this point I wondered how I could ever listen to anyone or anything else, or how I could let anyone disturb my peace. The mere thought of it seemed absurd.

———

I soon learned how naive that thought was. Sadly, after just five minutes of being back in Toronto, my dad pissed me off again. *Man, he gets to me!*

I had tried desperately to find a flight out of Ottawa so as to avoid seeing the parents (and because I was not ready to have them meet Dusty), but it just wasn't in the cards. I will spare you the details, but let's just say my dad was not impressed with Dusty's redneck accent and they clashed pretty much immediately.

> **take another look**
> **go ahead, you'll be fine**
> **it's good to see the world**
> **through a different kind of eye**
> **it's a matter of perspective**

a new one at that
so let your old one go
to enjoy a new flow

It really wasn't fair of me to subject him to my father, but doing so was cheaper than a hotel room and I thought we'd be able to manage it together as a team. In truth, I did *okay*. In future, I would have to do better, I told myself.

My parents didn't try to deter me from my decision, but those quick remarks and rolling eyes that communicated disapproval still irked me. Deep down, I guess I was still looking for approval. But mostly it was my reaction to them that bothered me. Frustration, anger, resentment…

I wondered what it was going to take to laugh it off and love them anyway.

part ii

fresh perspective

. . .

February 1998

I SAT at a table on the rooftop of my hotel, coffee in hand, waiting patiently for words as the crisp air blew against my cheek, blowing my busy mind away with it and leaving me in a state of wonder. I gazed in astonishment at the breathtaking view of the snow-covered Himalayas in the near distance.

I had never even entertained the idea of visiting Nepal until that first summer on the Ottawa River when Jerry had told me insane stories of his time there as a video kayaker. Ahh, Jerry. We had lost touch after that season, but since then I had often wondered what he was up to. We may not have had the kind of romance I had dreamed of in my mind, but I was forever grateful that he inspired me with his adventures in Taiwan and Nepal.

As you know, Taipei was a city of hustle. The grind. The traffic. The pollution and people and 7-Elevens. My relationship with it was a tumultuous one, filled with stress and tension in the battle for money. Always in the race against time. But here in Pokhara, I felt a state of grace. It was an innocent love, into which I was easily seduced. The kind smiles of the people, the intoxicating aromas of the food, and the majestic mountains where the rivers ran wild. I could slow down, relax, and breathe. Here, time extended.

And I had left Dusty in Taipei.

> **friends come and go**
> **it's all part of the flow**
> **so don't be afraid**
> **to let people go**
> **now move forward with love**
> **and remember what's true**
> **this world needs only**
> **the best version of you**

In truth, I was glad we had traveled together so early in our relationship simply to knock off what could've been years of slowly reaching the conclusion that we were not quite the right fit. It's better to know than be afraid to know, you know? So when in doubt, I highly recommend going for it. You'll either grow closer or more distant, but both are equally poignant page-turners in the book of your magnificent life.

Having traveled so much on my own already, I had been longing for a companion to share my adventures. Even desperate for it. Dusty managed to fill this void, at least temporarily. But the thing about voids, as I had come to learn, is that even with Dusty around I eventually began to feel alone. I realized that he was never going to be able to satisfy me in the way that I thought a partner would.

Nobody could.

I had begun toying with this idea around four weeks after our arrival at the hostel. My mind and heart were at odds, leaving me uncomfortably torn between two worlds. I waited it out, hoping for an inner reconciliation, but nothing changed, and I couldn't deny the fact that the adoration I had felt for him at the beginning had dissipated the more I got to know his childish ways.

It was nothing against him, truly. He was fun and kind and helpful, and he adored me in the way I had only previously dreamt about. I was finally having sex *and* orgasms frequently. Was the sex mind-blowing? With nothing to compare it with, I wasn't sure. Wouldn't I know if it was mind-blowing? I felt like I would.

I never thought I'd say this after having wanted it for so long, but the downside to regular sex was that I was beginning to feel that my body was not my own, that I was there to satiate his primal needs and that it was my duty to *give in* to those needs at least twice a day even though I didn't care to. I feared that he might cheat if I didn't. Sex was becoming more of a bother than a pleasure, and I wondered if this was what it was like for all women.

Sigh.

In any case, the more we settled into the Taiwan life, the more I saw his incompetence. Or was it my intolerance? Let's just call it *incompatibility*.

And so when the time came to plan for Thailand, I could not fathom the idea of spending more time babysitting him. I know it wasn't his fault that he hadn't traveled before. I didn't hold it against him. What I couldn't grasp was his inability to save money. In Taipei, it was the whole purpose of us being there!

I had come to terms with the fact that he was unlikely to pay me back for the plane ticket, which of course was majorly disappointing, but the real buzzkill was realizing that he wouldn't be able to travel on a shoestring if he didn't manage his money. Ultimately, this was non-negotiable for me. A dealbreaker. I felt like a complete asshole for being this way, but it was what it was. The truth of the matter? I wanted my freedom back.

There. I said it.

Red Fran took it hard. She was highly entertained by his positive, outgoing energy, and maybe it was nice to have someone else to listen to for a change. For me, the emotional strain of it all had become too large to ignore, which was good because it gave me the strength to be honest about how I felt so that I could turn wholeheartedly in the direction of what I wanted: to travel again on my own.

He took it well enough. It hurt, but he didn't fight it, reminding me once again that he was a really good guy with a good heart who meant well. He decided to stay in Taipei for a little while longer, which I thought would be good for him in terms of establishing some independence, not that my opinion mattered.

It's funny. I had had such a deep desire to travel with a lover, actually to just *have* a lover. I didn't imagine it would turn out like this. A failure? It certainly wasn't all that it was cracked up to be. At least not with him. Was it possible I had spent too much time dreaming up an impossible dream, a fairy tale that could never be realized in the actual real world with actual real humans?

Call me selfish, but I wanted to turn the attention back to me, myself, and I. No more compromise. Maybe I was being too harsh. Maybe I was overly guarded. Whatever it was, it had been diluting my experience, pulling me this way or that, off course, essentially, all for the sake of someone else's needs. I didn't like it! I was in my early twenties, at the very beginning of finding my own path.

Now that I'd traveled both solo and with a partner, I felt that the only way I could trust my footing was to do exactly what I wanted, when I wanted. Regardless of the outcome, whether a complete nightmare or total dream, I would be a hundred percent responsible for my actions. I would know myself. And that's what I wanted.

So here I was in Nepal, sitting contently in front of the Himalayas, $8000 richer, and proud of myself for leaving behind a place that had served its purpose and a relationship that had run its course. Tomorrow I would begin the Annapurna Circuit, a bright and shiny new chapter that I was ready to welcome with open arms.

The Annapurna Circuit is a trek within the Himalayas that encircles the Annapurna Massif. I think 'massif' means a bunch of peaks and valleys. Anyway, it's approximately 131 km and takes on average somewhere between 15-20 days depending on pace, weather, acclimatization days, side trips, etc. The trek crosses two different river valleys and reaches its highest point at Thorong La pass at a whopping 5416 meters.

I had no doubt it would be a challenge. The highest ascent I did on Mount Kenya was Point Lenana at 4985 meters and that was no small feat. We began at 4 a.m. and I remember being dizzy and out of breath with every step as we pushed forward in the dark, up the steep climb through snow and rock. It was scary and dangerous and that was without Red Fran on my back! When the sun emerged on the horizon, I clambered those last ten feet to the top as quickly as I could so that I could get to the monumental cross that marked the highest point and watch the sun fully present itself to the day. I remember it being freezing cold with howling winds, but the sky was clear and the view of the moun-tain range was glorious, lit with hues of orange and yellow and red.

It was well worth the effort.

This trip was going to be 122m higher and in a shorter time frame (by a few days in my approximation), but I knew I could do it. I mean, I just *would*. I was going, so I would *have* to, right?

Red Fran, of course, was ever the pessimist.

RF: "Um, you sure about this?"

Me: "Obviously."

RF: "Yeah but remember that time in Kenya when you tripped on a rock and almost fell off the side of the cliff?"

Me: "What? No way."

RF: "For real."

Me: "You're so full of shit."

RF: "I swear. That day we hiked to Simba Tarn."

Me: "...Simba Tarn, I forgot about that! But Fran, I didn't almost fall off a cliff. You're exaggerating. Try as you might, you're not getting out of this."

RF: "Sigh…"

I smiled at the memory of Simba Tarn, *simba* meaning lion, *tarn* meaning glacier lake, so named because a lion was spotted there, which didn't make sense at 4572m!

What adventures awaited this time?

annapurna circuit day 1

. . .

February 12, 1998: 1200M

LET'S just get something clear: jumping up and down blindfolded on the edge of a cliff was safer than riding the local bus in the mountains of Nepal. It was a terrifying seven-hour experience from Pokhara to Besisahar, the starting point for the Annapurna Circuit. We twisted and turned around narrow bends in the mountains, across ancient bridges and on a dirt road (if you could even call them 'roads') so narrow it could barely fit one bus. What would happen if we met an oncoming vehicle?

I prayed not to find out.

Truthfully, I spent most of the time anticipating what to do when the bus inevitably missed the bank in the turn and slipped off the cliff and how to save myself as I plunged to my death.

Before you ask, no, there was no such thing as railings here.

I looked around at the other passengers but nobody seemed concerned. They were all Nepalese locals, so this was just another day's commute for them. They sat contentedly with bags of grain, fruits, or babies on their laps. I don't know how I was the only foreigner, certain as I was that I'd meet up with some other trekkers on this death machine, eager to join forces for the hike. I was actually a little disappointed this was not the case.

I remember Jerry had told me that he and the other guides

would sit on the roof of the bus amongst the luggage so that they could jump off if need be.

"But you have to be careful of the electrical lines, Tish, 'cause they pop up out of nowhere and you better duck, or else..."

"Jesus, Jerry, I don't know about that..."

I now understood the appeal. At least on top of the bus, there would be some feeling of control, even if it was futile, whereas inside it you would most certainly go down with the ship. I'd been learning the importance of putting myself and my safety first, especially when traveling, and since these people seemed far less concerned about dying than I was, I made a mental note to strongly consider it on the next big bus ride. I'd have to survive this one first, of course.

In the meantime, all I could do was stare out the open window, focus on the grinding and repetitive Nepalese music blaring from the bus, inhale dirt and gas fumes, and pray.

> **focus less on tomorrow**
> **and more on today**
> **surrender your worries**
> **and let play dominate your day**

We got one flat tire along the way, but it didn't stop the driver from carrying on. Thankfully, we caught up to a truck that had broken down ahead of us, which forced him to stop and fix it since we couldn't go anywhere until the truck was on its way. Presumably. I don't actually know if anything was fixed. Through my hazy window I could see five others standing around the truck, hands gesturing as they discussed the problem.

I guess all that staring fixed it, because about an hour later everyone got back into their respective vehicles and off we went. The small, older Nepalese man sitting next to me with his chicken gave me a toothless smile. His eyes, clear and bright, seemed like they were laughing, and I got the sense that everything would be okay.

**your sweet peace of mind
comes from deep down inside
so stay true to your heart
to maintain that bright spark**

I exited the bus in Besisahar and was thrilled to see Red Fran when the guy on the roof threw the bags down. We were immediately accosted by men hustling us towards their restaurants inviting us in for a meal: "Please, good food, good price, this way." They gestured toward old shacks very near to where the bus stopped. I was starving so we followed an elderly man to his place, and sat down for a bite.

RF: "I thoroughly enjoyed that ride. It was very peaceful up there and the view was glorious."

Me: "Good for you. I was scared shitless."

RF: "Next time you should ride up top with me."

Me: "Yes. absolutely. I've already decided that."

RF: "By the way, you sure have a lot of stuff. Have you never thought of traveling light? What the fuck is all this?"

Me: "You know I don't like being cold."

RF: "You're gonna regret it."

I abhorred when Fran was right, and having to admit it was even worse, but on this rare occasion she was. After filling my belly, we began the trail. It was nice to be underway, on foot so that I could stretch my legs and move my body after that tense, uncomfortable ride. Unfortunately, it didn't take long before realizing my pack was dreadfully heavy and already a concern. Even though I'd packed as minimally as possible, I hated being cold so it was likely I was carrying a few more layers than the next guy. That was, if there was one.

RF: "I hate to say I told you so. Oh wait, no I don't."

Me: (struggling and grunting)

RF: "Just admit it. it's okay if you do. It doesn't make you any less of a person."

Me: "At least I'll always be more of a person than you!"

RF: "Ooooh that really hurts! Haha as if I care!"

Speaking of which, since I hadn't met any trekkers on the bus, I certainly hoped to meet up with some along the way. Somewhere. Somehow. I liked Red Fran and all, but she was a bit of a princess and therefore not the most supportive companion. As you could see by now, our personalities often clashed and I was concerned I would throw her off a bridge if it ended up being just the two of us the entire time.

As for bridges, we were currently crossing the first of many suspension bridges. This one was made of steel, but I heard there were some old wooden and roped ones along the way as well. It was a very narrow pedestrian-only bridge (as they all would be), which meant no vehicles. Yay! It was also a swinging one. If you liked roller coasters, this would not be an issue, but if you scared easily, it probably wasn't your cup of tea. Either way, you'd definitely be holding onto either side with both hands while crossing. Red Fran was not impressed.

RF: "Oh my God, oh my god, oh my god. Not looking down."

Me: "Wait, but the roof of the bus wasn't a problem?"

RF: (hyperventilating)

Me: "Close your eyes and stop shaking. You're pulling me off balance and making it worse. We're almost there, just focus on your breath."

RF: (still breathing heavily)

I looked at the Marshyangdi River below me. We would be criss-crossing this river valley the entire way up. One river, one mountain range, yet the terrain would continually change. I wondered if I'd stay the same or if, like the terrain, I'd also change.

Me: "Okay you can relax, we're on the other side."

RF: (trying to breathe normally again)

Me: "Um, you know we're going to be crossing like a ton of these, right?"

RF: (returning to heavy-breathing)

Me: "Oh my god. Calm down. You'll get better at it, I promise."

As the afternoon progressed, we passed dozens of local Nepalese men, who I gathered were making their way back to town. I couldn't even count how many times we said "hello", to which they would reply "Namaste", and shortly thereafter "give me pen", a common thing to ask from foreigners, I soon found.

It was a pleasant, introductory three hours to our destination: Bhulebule.

In bed at the Manang Hotel that evening, I was in a basic room overlooking the river. I say 'basic' to give a general sense of what to expect of the guest houses on this trek: rough wooden planks that are not seamlessly joined. Let's just say there were lots of small gaps in the walls.

In all honesty, it was a luxury to be on a trek where you walk from one tea house to another, with actual beds to sleep in and real food cooked for you instead of having to set up camp and cook freeze-dried food or rice. A luxury I could only have dreamed of on Mt. Kenya.

annapurna circuit day 2

· · ·

February 13, 1998, 1136M Syange

THE NEXT MORNING while eating some fresh eggs and bread, I marveled at the fact that there had been a satellite TV on during dinner the night before. I had a light in my room, and was awakened by a ringing telephone! Electricity? Crazy!

Red Fran, however, was having a moment.

RF: "Yesterday was brutal. I regret being forced into this trip. The days planned out in the Lonely Planet are impossible goals, and underestimate the difficulties. Up, up, up you go for *two* hours! Half of the restaurants and snack shops are closed because it's low season. I was starving the whole way up to Bahundanda from Ngadi. Then we go down, down, down, and..."

> all you need is within reach
> just have a look around
> see what's up and what's down
> in front and all around
> widen your view
> and you'll see all the beauty awaiting you

I interrupted.

Me: "Yes, we are already sore. And yes, it will be hard, but it *will* get better. We'll get stronger and it'll get easier. Besides, the tea house I want to get to in Syange apparently overlooks a beautiful waterfall!"

RF: "Hmpf. I'm not going to buy into your naive promises. I just hope our goal to get to Dharapani is an attainable one."

She was so melodramatic. But I needed her. How else would I carry around all my baggage?

annapurna circuit day 3

· · ·

February 14, 1998, 2000M Tal

I FELT strong and in good spirits, but just like these mountains had ups and downs, I knew my mind would too. It would be a game of keeping things in perspective.

RF: "Hey do you remember that day at the beginning on Mt. Kenya when you were wheezing so hard and that guy Ed called you a slow-ass bitch because you were slowing the group down?"

Me: "Your point?"

RF: "That was funny."

I remembered it all too well. My body felt good but my lungs were not on point, and I was wheezing almost to the point of hyperventilating. I could only go as fast as my lungs would let me, which was painfully slow. I was already frustrated, embarrassed, and feeling terrible for holding up the group. Ed didn't have to be a dick about it, but we would all have our shitty moments.

I don't know why Fran had brought that up right now. So far, it was my legs, not my lungs, that slowed me down. We were almost 2000m higher in elevation that day on Mt. Kenya. I think she was still having a hard time accepting what we were doing and was trying to psyche me out… or piss me off. Good thing for me I'd learned in Africa not to let her get to me.

We made it to Chamje for lunch, which meant we were on pace to meet our goal. The only passersby were the goats and donkeys. Mind you, the donkeys had poor awareness of personal space and couldn't care less about staying in their lane, which meant they were constantly pushing me off the trail.

RF: "Goddammit, those useless fuckers!"

Me: "Fran, can you chill out please? They're donkeys!"

The last bit of the day involved a hard, anger-inducing steep climb. My legs were shaking by the end of it. But at the top, we could see the town of Tal below, a picturesque village on a flat plain next to the river only a few kilometers away. Seeing that finish line gave me just the surge of energy I needed to shift my darkening thoughts to something more positive. Instead of focusing on my chaffed butt, which had led to me thinking about how fat my thighs and ass were, and how much easier it would be if I had that elusive thigh gap (told you it was getting dark), I was able to look up from the ground and turn my attention to the blue sky and the glorious waterfall pumping over the mountain.

And now, walking under the thick stone archway, an entrance gate of sorts, we entered the village of Tal.

annapurna circuit day 4

. . .

February 15, 1998, 2164M Danaque

WE WALKED PAST BAGARCHHAP, a former village that had been wiped out by a mudslide only a few years earlier in 1995. I could feel the darkness surrounding it. Imagine: one minute a thriving Nepalese village, the people carrying on as usual; and the next, a rumble. A horrid warning sign that would not likely give enough time before it turned into a roar, shaking the ground as the earth slid from the top of the hillside and onto the village. Buried. At best, dead on impact.

It was a grim picture. And afterwards, any proof of its existence was gone, covered by the earth. There was only a memorial for three Canadians who had been caught in the mudslide and lost their lives. Apparently six other trekkers and eleven villagers were killed too.

The hotel we were in—Hotel Tibetan—was new. The owners had had a hotel in Bagarchhap, but after it was destroyed, they moved here to Danaque, and began building this one. Even though the reasoning behind their new beginning was a sad one, I couldn't help but enjoy my beautifully crafted room and the aromatic scent of freshly cut wood. It was obvious they had put some loving energy into this place as its lines and details were far more accurate than the previous rooms I'd stayed in.

annapurna circuit day 5

. . .

February 16, 1998, Rest Day

I'D BEEN FEELING dizzy so decided to take a rest day to
acclimatize. The sun was spectacular all morning, a true gift from
God, and I was grateful to peel off layers of clothing and let her
rays warm my skin and kiss my face. I leaned back in my chair
and appreciated the moment in its entirety.

> **walk into your day**
> **with a light heart and a bright ray**
> **feeling fresh from the start**
> **you are confident and smart**

The days had been beautiful, of course, but also long and hard.
Plus, it was February. Winter in the Himalayas meant that as you
moved higher in elevation, the climate became more and more
harsh. There was still the potential for cold rain here, but soon it
would be snow, biting wind, and temps dropping well below
freezing as soon as the sun set behind the mountains. With over
3000m to go, it was going to get harder before it got easier.

RF: "Tish, I can promise you have no shortage of warm clothes
here. I should know with how stuffed I am. You're just going to
have to deal."

I was obviously not going to respond, but she was right. I *would* have to get over it because I wasn't turning back. Like Taiwan, I was committed to this decision. I wanted it, I chose it, and here I was in it.

In it to win it.

Since I was solo (we do not include Red Fran in such things), the owner invited me to eat with him and his family. I almost died of relief when I entered the kitchen and felt a wave of heat hit me.

The Nepalese eat four meals per day:

- Meal 1: tsampa porridge and tea
- Meal 2: dal bhat
- Meal 3: Tibetan bread with tea
- Meal 4: dal bhat

I'm not sure I'll ever tire of *dal bhat*. It's basically lentil soup served with rice and sometimes potato or vegetables or whatever is being served. It's simple, delicious, and vegetarian. And while I'm no longer vegetarian, when traveling in strange lands, I've found that meat dishes can be quite a mystery and also potentially dangerous to the stomach. (To be frank, my preference is to not eat meat, but my body was craving it this past summer so I succumbed while at River Run. Being preferential is also harder when you don't have your own kitchen, so turning to meat was just less of a hassle.) With the dal, it's a real treat not having to concern myself with eating questionable meat for the sake of being polite, only to be barfing up a lung a couple of hours later.

From what I gathered from our hilarious attempt at dinner communication, only the mother died in the mudslide. The father had these sunglasses that he wore even in the dark cement kitchen. He prayed all day long, but to me it just sounded like moaning, and he said two English words at dinner: "cat" and "goodnight". These, he yelled out to me accompanied by a big grin as I left the kitchen to go to bed.

My dizziness had subsided, my feet were nice and warm from the fire, and now I was cozied up in bed and happy, ready to set off again in the morning.

annapurna circuit day 6

. . .

February 17, 1998, 2615M Chame

IT WAS an early start to the day. The harsh wind was already hurting my face, and I wasn't sure I was up for the torture. Luckily, the clouds soon gave way to the sun and she graced us with the gloriousness of her warmth for the remainder of the day, easing my discomfort and enabling me to enjoy the experience, and the view, instead of hating on life.

Massive pine trees led the way, their needles covering the ground beneath them, reminding me of my summers spent at camp in northern Ontario.

Ah, camp. It was by far my most favorite part of childhood. Freedom, nature, sports, connection, friendship… Come to think of it, was that what I was continually trying to recreate in my adult life? River Run had certainly been in alignment with the camp-like experience. I'd say travel was somewhat similar.

Was I starting to understand what my dad meant by it's time to stop playing around and join the real world? He saw my life choices as me choosing camp. But was that a bad thing? Was that kind of lifestyle only supposed to be a fun experience contained to childhood summers? Man, he sure made the 'real world' seem like a drag. No wonder I resisted it.

Wait. What's that? Oh my God, there are voices behind us.

I turned around to see a group of three guys catching up to us! It was our first sight of other trekkers in a week! Their presence made me wonder if perhaps the map *was* a reasonable route and I was just terribly slow?

"Well, hello there!" one of the guys said as I made way for them to pass.

RF (whispering): "Don't let them pass, dude, pick up the pace!"

Me (whispering back): "Shh! Zip it!"

Truth be told, I did intend to keep up with them, though I knew I'd be working hard for it and that it would be best to let them pass and resign myself to being the straggler, hoping they'd put up with me.

The timing of their arrival turned out to be a blessing. Shortly thereafter, we had to traverse a sandy landslide, which evolved into sinking mud, all on an intimidatingly steep angle! I was thankful they waited around to make sure I got across safely.

Now in Chame, I was secretly stoked to be invited to stay at the same tea house as Ed, Stuart, and Sam. All Brits. All cunningly sarcastic Brits. I could not keep up. I had zero credit when it came to witty remarks and I was for sure a terrible disappointment with each attempt. Oh well. While it was nice to 'have Nepal to myself' up until today, I was relieved to have some buddies now that the trek was getting more intense.

Ironically, in high season, this circuit sees 200 trekkers a day where apparently everyone is in a daily race to the next destination so as to secure a bed for the night because accommodations are limited. This is particularly true nearer to the top where there might only be one or two tea houses. Can you imagine? What a circus that must be. Consequently, I've seen many tea houses under construction, which I suppose is good for the local economy, but maybe not so good for the environment or the trekkers' experience.

I may not love this freezing winter weather but I'd still choose it over the stress I'd feel with encountering hordes of people. I'm a fairly competitive person, but this was not the kind of competition I'd want to be in. In fact, I'd probably have zero appreciation for my surroundings because my head would be down, focused on getting from point A to point B. I'd surely die of altitude sickness for refusing to take acclimatization days.

That night, over another lovely dal bhat dinner, the guys shared some unnerving stories of the Thorong La pass, a long day up the mountain to its highest point, the pinnacle of the circuit, then a long descent down the other side. Stuart said they met some people in Pokhara the night before they left who apparently had to turn back because of snow blocks on the mountain covering the trail. Instead of continuing up, over, and down the other side, they had to come back the same way. In other words, it could take 12 hours if there was snow, and to be prepared for the biting and blinding wind that went with it.

I didn't like that story, especially when he promised it wasn't an exaggeration and apparently common at this time of year. Of course, I'd had no idea. I hadn't come to Nepal with the intention of doing the Annapurna Circuit so had no research under my belt. It was just what was in the flow. I came here, heard about it, it felt good, so...

Here I was.

annapurna circuit day 7

. . .

February 18, 1998, 3115M, Pisang

FUCKING TOUGH DAY. I was freezing cold and exhausted, treading through the calf-deep snow which only got worse when the afternoon sun softened the snow so that I was sinking up to my knees. It was the one time the sun was not on my side. I cried a lot. It was so frustrating and Stuart kept telling me to hurry up. What a pompous dick.

We stopped for lunch at a tea house and sat around the fire. Our socks and shoes rested on the rocks near the heat, hoping to dry them before heading out again. I couldn't help but stare menacingly at Stuart. If he could feel the daggers I was throwing at him in my mind, he'd be dead a hundred times over, his blood and guts spilled out and covering the floor.

RF: "Easy, killer. That's a bit harsh."

Me: "Hmpfff."

RF: "Is this really about him, or is this about how hard this is?"

Me (shrugging): "Hmpfff."

RF: "You know, there's a fine line between pushing yourself and punishing yourself."

Me: "You're just saying that because you want to turn around."

RF: "Hmpfff."

I was having a dark moment and hating my decision to be here. I went through the same thoughts on Mt. Kenya on *most* of the days. It was this massive mind-fuck of 'is this really worth the pain?' vs. 'look how awesome I am!'

Why do I keep torturing myself like this? I wondered. These mountain expeditions were really more fun after the fact, when you could look back and enjoy what was at times immense suffering.

RF: "That's why they call it 'Type II Fun'."

Me: "What?"

RF: "Yeah, Type I Fun is fun while it's happening. Just, basic fun like a good meal, or going for a dip in the lake. Or camp. Type II Fun is miserable while it's happening and fun in retrospect, like this shit. Type III Fun is not fun at all, not even in retrospect, like an abusive relationship."

Me: "Interesting. Well, that certainly didn't lighten the mood."

RF: "Hey man, that's on you."

While thawing out and waiting for our socks to dry, I turned my attention to Sam. He had a kind face, a pleasant manner, *and* he was friendly.

"So how did you end up here?" I asked.

"Oh, well, I've been here for a year, and spent time in both Manang and Tal. I'm a nurse, and wanted to see if I could be of service in these areas on the mountains."

"So you've helped a lot of people?"

"Well, I've done as much as I can with what I've got, at least for now. I might want to set up a non-profit or something to help get more nurses and supplies. Dunno yet. It's sad, really. The blokes here who get sick generally either wait to get better or wait to croak because the only proper treatment is in the city, which is too far away, and too expensive."

"Oh wow..."

I didn't know how to respond, though it did make me see that 'immense suffering' was not an accurate way to describe my experience on the mountain. Maybe it would be more accurate to say 'out of shape' or 'unprepared.' Perspective was everything, wasn't it?

> **sometimes I'm up**
> **sometimes I'm down**
> **but I'll always come around**
> **to the sweet feeling within.**
> **from darkness to light**
> **it's better to shine bright.**

I felt light-headed and short of breath as we continued on our way, though I dug deep to find hope that I would acclimatize well for tomorrow. A Danish couple came out of nowhere and flew past us! I swear there was nobody behind us for miles and then —*poof!* —there they were, smiling and waving their walking sticks in greeting as they made the pass. Seriously, they were so light on their feet it looked as though they were skipping through a field of daisies on a bright summer day.

Fuckers.

annapurna circuit day 8

. . .

February 19, 1998, 3352M, Manang

OUR DAY BEGAN with an immediately torturous and steep incline. The terrain leveled off, teasing me only briefly before turning into a gradual incline where we had to stomp through the once again knee-deep snow.

This thin air was killing me. I swear this was much harder than Kenya. Like, what the fuck? Maybe it was because I was busting my ass to keep up with the boys but I also wasn't inclined to slow down and be on my own again, not as the terrain got harder and more dubious with high altitude and unforgiving weather.

annapurna circuit day 9

. . .

February 20, 1998, 1176M, Lattar

WE CLIMBED 700m today and dare I say I actually felt good! The weather was spectacularly clear and sunny, enabling us to cover a lot of territory and I don't remember grumbling once. We saw snow leopard tracks, which was epic because, according to Ed, they were an endangered species. And there were horses at the lodge where we finished our day! I wouldn't have thought they'd be able to manage the thin air, but then again, I know nothing about horses.

There were eight of us now: me, the three Brits, the Danish couple, and two Swedish dudes. Thankfully, we were all having fun together though Stuart and I were still at odds. I finally told him off last night for being a misogynistic prick. I'm not one to throw out labels because in all fairness, he might just be a prick in the most general sense, but I hadn't heard him say mean things to the others which made it feel very personal. The tipping point was when he said that I ate like a fat cow so it was no wonder I couldn't get a boyfriend.

RF: "Oh shit, here we go."

"Hey man, who the fuck do you think you are talking to me like that? I may be slow and sometimes miserable, but I'm frustrated. It's hard keeping up with you guys but I want to stick with you and you don't have to be such a prick about it. Walk ahead if you don't want me around. And by the way, you remind me of George Costanza so I don't know what right you think you have trying to knock me down. Can't you see I'm already down? What, do I remind you of a girlfriend who dumped your ass when she found out what a prick you were? Or maybe you're just bummed because I remind you of someone you liked but she'd have nothing to do with you because, again, you're an arrogant, mean piece of shit who gets his thrills trying to make nice people feel bad about who they are because you're so miserable yourself ..."

Welcome to the dark side of my personality. I'll keep quiet and take it and let things slide and 'behave' and try to not take it personally... until I've had enough. Then, one last remark and the dragon unleashes and the truth of how I feel comes flying out of my mouth like fire. It's the strangest thing. I don't even know where it's coming from. It's like it's not even me. After it happens, I'm just as surprised as everyone else. In fact, nobody, *especially* me, would be expecting *that*.

When this happens, my surprise inevitably turns to fear because: what the hell did I just do and have I been horribly mean? I look around, the 'audience' in front of me staring silently, their jaws dropped in awe. Then when their shock turns into bellowing 'ohhhh yeah!' followed by laughter, and then clapping, my fear turns into relief. All is well in the world, like I brought balance back to the fucked-up human equation of what I don't know. It's weird but true, I promise. It's happened on more than one occasion and the result has always been the same.

The Brits' reactions were no different, including Stuart. In fact, he was laughing the most! Maybe they were just happy to see some of my personality come through? It makes me wonder if I spent too much time in my head and not enough time laughing and allowing myself to be happy.

RF: "Well, you are a very serious one."

Me: "Me? I thought you were the one with the crabby attitude."

RF: "I didn't say crabby. I said serious. There's a difference. But thanks for the insult. You like to go on all these adventures, but then sometimes you don't let yourself enjoy them. You're all wrapped up in your head and beating up on yourself for not being good enough. I, on the other hand, am happily crabby. It's part of my charm!"

Me: "Huh."

Either way, it seemed as though I'd gained some cred with these guys. Props to me I guess, but I didn't know why they needed to hear me roar in the first place. It reminded me of my mom, always holding her tongue so as not to wake the monster (my dad). Apparently, I was doing the same thing. But I was thinking it wasn't the right thing to do. Or at least it wasn't how I wanted to be. Pretending to be okay and staying silent when you feel hurt by someone else's words is a disservice. Plus, by not expressing myself in the moment, I wasn't letting people get to know me. Did that mean I was afraid of being seen? And if so, why?

RF: "Because you're afraid you won't be liked for who you are."

Me: "Ughhhh. Dammit!"

RF: "It makes sense as to why you have a hard time attracting romance. You're pretty closed off even though you want it."

Me: "…who *are* you right now?"

RF: "Hey, I can be learning too. I know I can be a drag, but I *am* glad I'm here you know."

Me: "Wow. That's the nicest thing you've ever said."

RF: "BTW, that rant on Stu was mind-blowing… best part of my day!"

Me: "Cool. Thanks for having my back!"

RF: "Dude, how could I not *have* your back when I'm always *on* your back?"

annapurna circuit day 10

. . .

February 21, 1998, 4358M, Phedi

THE WEATHER WAS HORRENDOUS TODAY. Snow and cloud cover. My toes and fingers were numb all day and all I could think about was getting across the pass where it would be all downhill from there. In a good way.

The pass had become less intimidating to me now that I knew I'd have others to conquer it with. Even the Danes and the Swedes who were off and running during the day waited for us in the afternoon, cheering us on, beers in hand as we approached them, exhausted and ready to rest. Truth be told, they could have easily been down the other side by now. I was grateful for their support.

Since my outburst, things between Stu and I lightened up. I felt clearer, more confident, and open to real conversation. With less resistance, it felt, dare I say, friendly. Ed and Sam have always been super sweet, genuinely upbeat and chill. It has been a fucking blessing to join with them and they promised me they were in no rush so I never worried about slowing them down.

Who knows? Maybe I didn't slow them down and it was all just in my head?

Life is weird.

annapurna circuit day 11

. . .

February 22, 1998, Rest Day

THE BRITS and I rested and acclimatized for the big day tomorrow. It was finally here, the Thorong La pass. If this were a music festival, this would have been the headliner. All the previous days were opening acts; the ones to follow, the afterparty.

The Danes and the Swedes, however, left for the pass this morning because they were robots and robots don't need time to acclimatize. The sun was shining and the sky was clear blue. And —miracle—we could actually see the pass in front of us. It was an intimidating sight: desolation, dirt, rock, steep. We were cornered by this mountain now; the only way out was up and over.

In other random news:

A Korean monk whose name was either Sue or Sua (she's so quiet that I'm having a hard time deciphering her words) arrived today.

The toilet here was atrocious; a shed with a hole in the middle of it, which was like all the others except that this one was piled to the brim with frozen poop. Yep. It didn't ever get a chance to decompose in this frigid weather so it just piled up, along with the toilet paper thrown into the corner of the shed. Gnarly stuff.

A yak here was worth 15,000 Nepalese rupees and the guy

who runs this tea house had 28 of them. A snow leopard killed a baby yak the other day, but apparently the leopards just drank the blood and didn't touch the meat.

We were planning to leave the next day at 6 a.m., hoping to reach the top by noon. From there it would be four hours down to Muktinath. Ten hours total. Pray for me.

annapurna circuit day 12

. . .

IT WAS STILL DARK when we started: the three Brits, the Korean, and me. We were all quiet as we ate porridge at 4:30 a.m. I was already nervous and therefore had no appetite but forced down the food because I knew I would need it. I had saved a Mars bar in a special pocket in Red Fran that I bought in Pokhara and swore I wouldn't touch it until I reached the top. My reward. We filled our water bottles and began at 5:30 a.m.

Up, up, and up we went as the snow continued to fall. Every time we thought we were near the top it was just a brief plateau before another incline. This went on for hours and it seemed like we'd never get there. By hour three, the winds were fierce, and it turned into a full-on blizzard. I had to fight hard not to get blown over. Red Fran was so heavy and the wind kept trying to take hold of her. It was a constant battle.

RF: "Steady onward. One step at a time, Tish!"

Me (panting): "Dying."

RF: "Keep moving forward!"

She was yelling while I was barely walking, then a gust of

wind would hit me and all I could do was stand there trying to hold my ground and wait for the gust to pass. Do you know how hard it was to push against nature? It was a goddamn force.

At 9 a.m., we lost the trail.

The blizzard had covered the trail in snow and it was no longer visible. We didn't have maps or compasses or anything. We were depending solely on the worn track in the dirt made by the thousands of other trekkers who had gone before us. But now, nothing. Just blinding snow and bare mountains on all sides. The only landmark would be the prayer flags symbolizing the peak, but nothing until then, and at this point the flags could be in any direction. I broke down in tears. I was sobbing and didn't care because I knew nobody would be able to hear me over the howling winds. We were together, but on our own. Just like life, I suppose.

Lost, with no trail to follow back and no trail to follow forward, I thought we might actually die. How long would it be before our bodies were discovered by another wandering traveler? It could be days, or months, or years, depending upon how far off track we'd gone. I've done a lot of stupid things that had scared me in the past, but nothing compared to the fear I felt right now, because right now, for the first time in my life, I knew what it felt like not to have the strength to go on.

I was on the brink of giving up.

Thank God, I wasn't alone. And thank God for Ed, who turned into our pack leader and kept pushing us all on despite the fact that we didn't know if we were headed in the right direction.

> **listen to your heart**
> **it knows the way**
> **let it speak to your mind**
> **so you know what direction to take**

Even Stuart stuck close to me, yelling out words of encouragement that ended up turning into a confession of some sort.

"Tish, mate, no giving up," he said. Then a few steps later, "Tish, we're going to celebrate tonight with a pint." A few more steps, "Tish, I know I've been a dick. I'm sorry." And then finally, "Tish, I've had some shite going on at home that I haven't... Well, maybe I am starting to... I've been angry. I'm sorry you became my target. I didn't mean it. I don't even know why..."

He was huffing and puffing between words, yelling into the winds just enough so that I could hear him. Honestly, I don't know how he was managing to talk without his tongue freezing off. My face was tucked deep in my jacket, and while I wanted to respond and let him know I heard him, I simply couldn't.

At 10:30 a.m., the blizzard lifted! Even better, within a few minutes of the blizzard lifting, Ed spotted the path ten feet to our left. I had been sure we were walking into our death, but maybe, just maybe, we were walking up to life.

Now I knew what miracles felt like.

At 11 a.m., the Korean monk got altitude sickness. She was buckled over and retching. She had refused a rest day and therefore had not acclimatized in Manang. I'm guessing she didn't want to wait to do the pass alone and that was why she forewent the acclimatization day in order to join us. We had to be closer to the top than we were to our starting point, so Ed convinced her to drop her pack and go up and over with us.

By 12:30 p.m., the skies were a dull gray in color but we were glad to still have visibility. As we came over another peak to yet another plateau, there, just a little bit higher, in the near distance, Tibetan prayer flags fluttered in the wind. The elusive peak was finally within reach!

I bawled my eyes out all the way to the flags and stumbled up to Stuart who had gotten there a few minutes prior and gave him a big hug. He opened his arms to return the embrace.

"I heard everything you said, Stu. Thank you."

There's no word that could accurately describe how I felt in that moment as we hugged it out. Anything I thought of fell painfully short. All I can say is I was thankful to be alive, knowing I was definitely not ready to die.

> **relationships are sacred**
> **with beautiful lessons to learn**
> **when we give love through forgiveness**
> **everyone is heard**

We stood at the peak and took in the colorful rectangles of cloth strung along many such trails and peaks high in the Himalayas. The Tibetans believe the prayers and mantras written on them would be blown by the wind to spread goodwill and compassion throughout the area. In that moment, we all felt the depth of the meaning that those flags carried.

We put our bags down to drink some water, and I took off my mitts and dug into the special side pocket of Red Fran to surprise everyone with my Mars bar. Treats such as this one were not available after Day 3, so it was kind of a big deal.

"Guess what I have for us?" I said, as I tried to pull on the zipper of the pocket. But my hands were numb and stiff and not able to pinch the zipper pull.

"Let me get that for you, mate."

Stu gestured for me to put my hands back in my mitts before he quickly unzipped the pocket, pulled out the Mars bar and waved it in front of everyone. He was laughing.

"OH MY GOD! IS THAT A MARS BAR?" Sam asked, very enthusiastic.

"It is, yes!" Stuart replied.

He was about to open it when he realized something.

"Oops, looks like a mouse may have gotten a wee bit of a head start though..."

"Are you fucking kidding me???"

I grabbed it with my mitts and inspected it. He was right. Everyone started laughing hysterically, a bit of much-needed comic relief, I suppose.

"Tish, it's just a wee mouse, he only ate a smidge."

Stu took it back out of my hand, opened it, broke off a piece for me, took a bit for himself and then passed it along.

Me (whispering to RF): "What the fuck? Why didn't you tell me?"

RF: "Too scared. Didn't want to bum you out."

Me: "Geez, you sure have become more thoughtful on this trip, haven't you?"

RF: "Am I? I promise it's not on purpose."

I wanted so badly to enjoy that chocolate bar, but the nause-ating altitude made it hard to swallow water, let alone eat chocolate.

The view of the mountain vista was probably a spectacular one, but sadly we couldn't see beyond 30ft, such was the dense gray atmosphere. We didn't linger for long as it was painfully cold, and Sua in particular needed to get to lower altitude ASAP. I was glad to get going as well, thinking the descent would be easy peasy.

But, shocker, it was not. As we descended and the weather lifted, all that new snow became softer and softer. Before we knew it, we were knee-deep in it for at least a full two hours. Every step was hard work.

At 3:30 p.m., the terrain finally became more manageable and the skies cleared, although there was still plenty of downhill to do, which I discovered was hard on the knees, especially with Red Fran on my back.

Finally, around 5:30 p.m., we arrived at the Bob Marley Guest House in Muktinath, exhausted beyond belief. Aside from some porridge at 5 a.m. and a tiny morsel of the Mars bar, I hadn't been able to stomach anything. Finally, I was hungry and happy!

The last 12 hours, seven of which were the climb to the top, were the hardest day of my life. I'm forever grateful to the Brits and truly thrilled to be alive.

annapurna circuit day 13

. . .

February 24, 1998, Rest Day

I SLEPT HARD LAST NIGHT, even amongst the snoring Brits. Today we took a rest day, and sat at the long dining table keeping warm by the fire and continually ordering food. Even though I was eager to get to a warmer climate, my body desperately needed a day to recover.

annapurna circuit day 14

. . .

February 25, 1998, 2665M, Marpha

THE DANES and Swedes had flown the coop, which wasn't surprising as I'm sure they had better things to do than wait around for us. Hopefully, we would catch up with them in Pokhara but you never know.

The Brits walked ahead today and I stayed back with Sua who was feeling much better, but still walking at an even slower pace than me. We eventually found them at a nice tea house called the Paradise Guest House. Everyone had already had a hot shower and I was so excited to get mine as it would be the first one since we started. But no, it turned cold after 30 seconds. I stood in the shower stall and cried while cold water dribbled down my head and fell on my skin, making me shiver.

The good news was we finally made it out of the snow today, woohoo!!! Fuck winter! I hate it! Entering this new landscape was surreal. Walking through Jomsom was like being in the Sahara Desert. The wind, unfortunately, did not have our back, so every step was a battle, dirt hitting us like little pellets shot out of a gun. Our faces were completely filthy by the time we got here so that I had no choice except to complete my frigid shower.

We had a happy dinner together and I got drunk on the smallest amount of apple brandy.

annapurna circuit day 15

. . .

February 26, 1998, 2560M - Kalopani

LONG WALK, everybody's muscles are sore.

annapurna circuit day 16

. . .

February 27, 1998, Tatopani

LONG HARD DAY of fast walking. After seven hours, we finally made it to the hot springs, a popular destination for people doing shorter treks around the lower Annapurnas, which explained the crowds.

It was interesting to hear people talk about their little 'treks'. Coming from what we'd just done, and were still doing, the notes just don't compare. I'm not trying to minimize their experience, but it did help me to realize that I'd fully maximized mine. Yes, it had been hard and painful and agonizing and I'd hated a lot of it... but I guess that's what made it so rewarding.

Type II Fun. There it is.

They say that freedom is on the other side of difficult things, but do we really need pain to feel pleasure or satisfaction? I would hate to think that was true, even though this experience was living proof of it, just like that day I got beat down multiple times in Phil's Hole before finally kayaking it successfully, or coming home alive every day after driving around Taipei on my moped.

Dinner, laughs, drunk on one beer.

Bed.

annapurna circuit day 17

. . .

February 28, 1998, Pokhara - 822M

I MADE IT!

After six and a half hours of walking along a trail on a ridge or over swinging bridges crisscrossing the Kali Gandaki Gorge, I finally made it.

The further down we went, the more yaks and locals we passed. Despite my blistered toes, I was upbeat in my anticipation to get to Beni, the finish line. Sua had stayed longer at the hot springs, so it was just me and the boys now. Red Fran was getting heavier and heavier each day after the pass, because I didn't need to wear as many layers. Yet I didn't complain, not once, at least not around the Brits. I liked them all too much and we had found some nice synergy between us. Stu and I had completely shifted our dynamic towards one another, going from disdain to respect.

> it's a glorious choice
> to use your great voice
> so be clear on the matter
> use love to break old patterns
> it takes practice and strength
> but I know you've got what it takes
> so go forth with your mind

and always be kind!

At the end, the trail led into a small village. Walking on the narrow dirt path with shacks on either side of us, it was the most civilization we had seen since Bhulbhule on Day 1. All eyes were fixated on us, as we were probably the most interesting thing walking by that day. Or maybe we just smelled bad.

We continued along the trail until it opened up into a bus and taxi area. The Nepalese locals crowded around us, yelling, presumably about where the buses were going. Ed found our bus to Pokhara leaving in an hour at 4 p.m. Good timing.

I was too tired to sit atop the bus for two hours. Sitting inside, I didn't even take notice of whether or not we were narrowly avoiding death at every corner, such was the daze I was in. I must have passed out, because before I knew it Ed was nudging me awake.

giardia in pokhara day 18

. . .

WOKE UP WITH GIARDIA. Awesome. At least I assumed it was giardia, since that was the common sickness amongst travelers around here. Giardia is an intestinal infection caused by tiny parasites found in food, water, or other surfaces that have been contaminated with poop from other infected people or animals. It's common in these parts because of the poor sanitation and, when ingested, causes diarrhea, cramps, and… Well, basically, it's best to be near a toilet. Thank God I was now at the Hotel Nirvana, where I had my own room and bathroom! Can you imagine if I was still on the trail and having to hike like this? Or worse. What if I was stuck having to squat over that horrifying hole of frozen shit in Phedi?

I didn't even care that I had it because I'm so glad I got it *after* the trek. And hey, maybe I'd lose a few pounds to add to the few pounds I'd lost since Day 1. So that was good…

It looked like I'd be here reading, sleeping, and pooping for the next few days or for as long as I needed, thank you very much.

long live the brits

. . .

IT TOOK a solid week to recover. I read, slept, relaxed, and basked in the comforts of the luxury of a real bed, and private bathroom with a hot shower and flushing toilet.

The Brits left for home a few days ago, and while I didn't get to spend time with them doing mini hikes and other fun adventures in Pokhara as we had discussed while soaking in the hot springs in Tatopani, I was glad to at least been well enough to spend a few hours with them on the night before their departure.

"Tish, mate, what are you going to do without us?"

By the tone of his voice, Stu seemed truly bummed about it. While I was confined to my room, he had been checking in on me every day, bringing me water, juice, bread, and other recovery essentials, like pills for giardia. (Though who really knew what they were, as he had bought them at the 'pharmacy', which was just a dude in a shack pretending to know what's up.) I had tried at the beginning to get my own supplies, stubborn as I was, but didn't get more than 20 feet before having to sprint back to the toilet. I had had no choice but to accept help, embarrassing as it was.

"Surprisingly, I may actually miss you too," I said with a smirk.

I had made the tiniest of improvements in my wit over the last couple of weeks, and combined with their very, *very* low expectations in my ability for humor, they took what they could get and we all managed to laugh at even my most lackluster attempts.

"But in all fairness, I'm so glad I forced myself to keep up with you on that bloody circuit. Painful as it was, guaranteed it was way more fun than it would've been if I had to get over that pass on my own..."

"Nah, mate, you would've had a grand time with Sua! Maybe she would've actually taken a rest day since you surely would've been a day behind us!"

"Huh. You're probably right about that, Sam."

"I think what Sam's trying to say is: you are most welcome!" Ed added, always the polite man of wisdom, keeping everyone in check.

We ate dinner at the Moonlight Restaurant while Titanic played on the TV in the background. As hard as it was, I gave Leo very little attention. I only had these guys for a couple more hours...

just the two of us

• • •

ON MY OWN AGAIN.

RF: "Hey! I resent that remark."

Me: "Well, you sort of count, but not really."

RF: "Um, I've been your only constant companion!"

Me: "More like a constant drag…"

While we rarely agreed on anything, one thing we were both glad for was to unpack all that warm gear and travel light again.

RF: "No. Light*er*."

Me: "Seriously?"

RF: "Girl, let's just say you are overly prepared when it comes to things you *might* need."

Me: "It's called safety preparedness."

RF: "It's called paranoia. Tell me honestly, do you really need two water bottles?"

Me: "What if I lose one?"

RF: "Exactly my point."

Me: "Ugh."

Now that I was mostly back to normal ('normal' being a relative term since diarrhea and other stomach issues were a given when it came to being a dirty backpacker in Southeast Asia where 'hygiene' was also a relative term), I was ready for my next adventure.

I was going to kayak the Kali Gandaki River, a five-day trip where I would be paddling alongside a rafting company. They don't usually accept random kayakers, but I just so happened to pop by that same day to see if I could somehow join their trip and somehow convinced them I wouldn't be a problem. Apparently, I could be very convincing.

RF: "It's just because you're a chick."

Me: "I hope so. The trip manager is a hottie. My only concern is that I've only been paddling for a year and a half and not sure if my skills will match up to the difficulty of the river."

This was one of those times where part of me knew I wasn't actually ready for this, but the other part of me didn't care. One might ask how it was that I got myself into sticky situations. Well, here we were: me thrill-seeking regardless of its level of stupidity because apparently in my world, adventure and safety don't coexist.

Still, something about it felt right and that's where I wanted to focus my attention.

> connect with the divine
> 'mmmhmmm' says my mind!
> she makes me feel good
> as I feel for her flow
> trusting her guidance
> because she's in the know

Red Fran, of course, didn't agree.

RF: "Yep, this is pretty stupid, and we're going to find out just how stupid."

Me: "You won't. You're staying behind."

RF: "Oh, thank God."

Red Fran hated getting wet, so she'd be staying at the head-quarters of Equator Rafting in Pokhara, while the minimal stuff I was bringing would be packed in a dry bag and kept in one of the rafts. I remembered how it had rained for a few days straight at the beginning of our Mt. Kenya climb and she was miserable. She may have been good for a lot of things, but getting wet was not one of them.

kali gandaki river day 1

. . .

I SAT on the roof of the bus on the one-and-a-half-hour drive to the put-in with some of the crew and I can confirm it was much better than being inside the bus. And yes, it may have been a false sense of security because it would still be a death-defying experience no matter what, but I would absolutely do it again.

While the crew unloaded the rafts and gear from the bus and got everything ready, I observed the clients. Did they realize how dangerous this could be, a trip on a remote river? Did they realize they were putting the safety of their lives in the hands of others? I doubted it. And yet I recognized myself in them, in their pure excitement for adventure, devoid of potential problems. Except for right now.

Right then I was having a moment, the kind of moment when something seemed like such a good idea in your head, but then when the time came for the actual 'doing' of it, you were like: *What the fuck was I thinking? Maybe I should turn around and make a run for it.*

A wave of guilt flooded my brain. I had been so focused on what *I* wanted that I hadn't stopped to think of what kind of danger I was putting the staff in, considering I'd never paddled anything other than the Ottawa River and hadn't even set foot in a boat in five months. I certainly didn't want to be a liability... I had to get my mind in the game. I had to decide that my presence would be helpful instead of harmful.

Kayaking was the *worst* sport to be nervous in, because if you're nervous, you tense up and become stiff, and when you become stiff, you're likely to catch an edge and flip. With unfamiliar continuous rapids, this meant having to navigate moment to moment, section by section. I had no idea what to expect except that I *couldn't* expect others to save me if I swam.

There was a fine line between being a hero and being dead and I wasn't sure where I sat on this line. I threw my kayak over my shoulder, grabbed my gear, and headed to the water's edge. I don't know if I mentioned this before, but Dusty and I had actually traveled with our kayaks and gear from Canada with the intention of coming here. Dealing with so much bulky equipment was a mission and a half but I hoped it'd be worth it.

Geared up and in my boat, I paddled around in the light current, getting comfy and re-familiarizing myself with kayaking, warming up with a variety of strokes. Kyle and Steve, the other two safety kayakers, paddled up to me and told me to stick with them and paddle ahead of the group to scout the first rapid, Little Brother. Phew! Normally, Dusty was my guide and coach so this was a huge first for me. I didn't foresee how insecure I'd feel doing this on my own, so I was appreciative they didn't take off without me.

We scouted it briefly, but I quickly got the gist of what I needed to do. I was a little shaky at the start but managed to get through upright. Good. The nerves were dusted off. The next rapid was Big Brother. We got out on shore at the top of the rapid and had a look at what was below. It was bigger.

Steve pointed out the line.

"Start left and move right, and avoid that hole in the middle."

Looked do-able from what I could see, and Kyle said I could

follow him down if I wanted. The thing with rapids is, it's easy to see your 'line' from shore, but once you're in your boat, all you see is a horizon line. If you don't give yourself landmarks to gauge where you are, how far from shore you want to be, and so on, it's kind of hard to know if you're 'on line' or not. I was nervous again and decided to follow Kyle so that I wouldn't have to think for myself.

In hindsight that was a really dumb move, because doing that strips you of your self-confidence.

I'd learned from experience with Dusty that I would need three paddle strokes to his one due to the difference in degrees of strength. You could never follow anyone precisely, due to everything being so dynamic. In any case, as soon as Kyle went over the horizon line, I was too focused on getting to him and not enough focused on where I was. I got all confused and found myself headed straight for a massive boulder. I leaned away from it—upstream, in other words—caught an edge and flipped over.

So there I was, upside-down, halfway through the first decent-sized rapid like a proper fool.

The rules of kayaking can be counterintuitive. I should have leaned *into* the rock like when a football player tackles his opponent, which unfortunately goes against human instinct when it comes to avoiding death.

I tried to roll numerous times, which is also counterintuitive to our survival instinct which would have you get out of your boat to get air immediately. So hey, maybe I get some points for not bailing right away. Still, bouncing around upside down, while knowing I was moving quickly downstream made it impossible to catch a breath. It didn't take long before I was out of air, not to mention hope. This swiftly led to panic, which inevitably led to pulling the plug.

Goddamit, fuck, fuck, fuck! I thought as I pushed myself out of my kayak.

At least I had the awareness to hold onto my boat and paddle, otherwise it would have been a massive shit show, because Kyle and Steve would be the ones to chase everything down and that was not their job.

One of them, I think Kyle, was yelling at me, "Swim right! Swim right!"

I struggled to make progress, what with all my gear. At some point, Steve paddled up to me and grabbed my boat, clipped it onto his tow rope and towed it to shore while I dealt with myself and my paddle. When he reached shore, he quickly unhooked my boat and, without looking at me, saying a word or asking if I was okay, went back to the top of the eddy to wait for the rafts.

I didn't think any of the raft guides had seen what happened, but waiting at the top of the rapid, they were probably wondering what was taking so long to get the sign it was safe to go (the 'high' sign of a paddle raised high in the air). The rafts came down one at a time, all safely, while I was back in my boat pretending as if nothing had happened.

Swimming a rapid was always humbling and embarrassing, but more importantly it was dangerous. I was ashamed I had already put other people at risk. Unacceptable. I vowed to get my head on straight for the rest of the trip. I was fully capable of kayaking this river, technically speaking. Dusty had done some research on rivers in Nepal and had explained this one to me back in Taiwan. He had felt that it was one I could handle, so even though I didn't know the specifics of each rapid, I knew, at least, that he had had faith in my ability. I just had to have faith in myself.

The weird thing about kayaking is that in the beginning you really do rely on people who are better than you. They are the ones who are there to rescue you, to help you scout and pick lines through a rapid, and to tell you which ones you are better off walking around. It's a necessary part of the process, because it takes a while to understand your own limitations, and ability to read the water.

I didn't have anyone else to rely on out here, though, so I had to wake the fuck up and take charge of myself. Every decision I made on the river is an important one. I decided right then and there to focus on my confidence, skill, and instinct instead of my lingering doubt.

> **let go of the old**
> **to make room for what's new**
> **you've got what it takes**
> **just believe...now it's true!**

What a difference mindset makes.

Making my way downriver, I focused on relaxing, loosening my hips, taking my time paddling from one section to another, pausing behind boulders where I could regroup, see what was below and pick my next line. Kyle forewarned me of the one bigger rapid I needed to be prepared for, and when we came to it, I breezed right through with no issues. Thank God.

By the time we pulled up to our camping spot mid-afternoon, my head was fully in the game. Relieved and excited to have survived Day 1, I eagerly gave the crew a hand pulling the rafts onto the beach and unloading the gear, set up my own tent, and then went back to chop veggies and help prep dinner. Now that I wasn't totally absorbed in myself, I was able to extend some of my energy elsewhere and wanted to be as helpful as possible.

When dinner was ready, we sat around the campfire eating off of plastic plates on our laps while Liam, the trip leader, shared some important intel on the culture of Nepal:

"So you've had a wee taste of what it feels like to ride the river's pulse, to be splashed by water that has traveled from high up in these mountains we admire as our backdrop, with miles and miles still to go... She's a beauty!"

With that Irish accent, he was a sexy one. He had long, dark ginger dreadlocks and a red beard with sun-kissed freckled skin that made the whites of his eyes pop, almost glowing as the light from the fire reflected his face. He was tall and lean, and as comfortable in this setting as if he'd been living like a caveman his entire life. But yeah, it was definitely his Irish accent that tied it all together into one big beautiful human. At least, I thought it was Irish.

"Nepal's traditions run deep, stemming from a history comprised of both kindness and violence. Such is humanity, is it not?"

I looked around and saw that everyone's eyes were glued to him. A few people nodded in agreement while others just continued to stare, waiting for what was coming next.

"For now, for tonight, I want to share my top ten things to know, if you don't already:

One, Sanskrit is the language of India, and is considered the oldest language in the world, 5000 years before Christ.

Two, Namaste is the standard greeting in Nepal. It can mean hello, goodbye, or thank you. The word comes from Sanskrit and translates to 'I salute the God in you' or 'I bow to you'. No doubt you've seen people put their palms together and then bow their heads, and say 'Namaste'."

"Where is he from?" I whispered to Kyle.

"Ireland," he replied.

"Nice. That's what I thought."

"Three, Nepali is the chief language. There are many ethnic groups and they speak hundreds of different languages. Not accents, or dialects, but languages. Sometimes Nepali people can't even communicate with one another!

Four, Hinduism and Buddhism are the two main religions."

He was a captivating, natural storyteller and I couldn't take my eyes off of him.

"Five, cows are sacred in the Hindu religion and cannot be killed. Coincidentally, their manure is also considered sacred, and it is common practice to clean and bless the home with water and cow manure. Once a cow stops producing milk, they are often released and the community is

responsible for feeding her. That's why they roam all over Nepal, even in the busy city of Kathmandu.

Six, Nepal has the only living goddess in the world, the Kumari. Kumari means virgin in Nepali and is the tradition of worshiping young pre-pubescent girls as manifestations of the divine female energy in Hindu religious traditions."

At this point, he paused to fill a pipe with tobacco, while we were forced to wait patiently. He picked up a small stick from the fire and lit the pipe, puffing on it gently. When its sweet scent of cherry reached my nostrils, I inhaled deeply, taking it all in, taking *him* all in, becoming more enthralled by the minute. Finally, he continued:

"Seven, about 90% of marriages in Nepal are arranged and the bride and groom will usually not meet or see each other before the wedding day —although 'love' marriages are becoming slightly more popular.

Eight, most of the power in Nepal comes from hydro-power, but it is not very reliable.

Nine, marijuana plants grow in gardens, on the side of the road, in ditches, on mountainsides. It's everywhere in Nepal."

I was drinking him in like a freshman crushing on a senior. His jawline, his hair, and he had this witchy...or warlock, rather, vibe. A warlock disguised in a flannel shirt. And in all fairness, it's pretty impossible not to fall for a good leader, especially when he's a mountain man such as this.

"And ten, the Nepal flag is the only national flag not quadrilateral in shape. It is made of two triangles. The triangles are said to represent Hinduism and Buddhism. They also represent the Himalayan Mountains.

And for your bonus fact, the abominable snowman, also known as the yeti, is a legendary apelike creature that is believed to frequent the high valleys of Nepal."

From leaving a relationship, to hiking the Annapurna Circuit, to recovering from giardia, it was clear to me that I'd gone through a lot. None of it was easy in the moment, but as I reflected on it that night in my tent, I was able to grasp just how worth it everything had been, because of how it had transformed me. I was stronger within myself, capable of overcoming obstacles, and content to be on my own, though more open to love. I felt better in my body and better in my mind.

I felt it was time.

kali gandaki river day 2

· · ·

WHERE THE OTTAWA RIVER was an oasis of peace, the Kali Gandaki was an elixir of magic. The Himalayas in the distant background magnified the remoteness, reminding me constantly of what a unique experience it was to explore the world via rafts and kayaks. Children waved to us enthusiastically from swinging bridges as we floated by underneath them. Women looked up from river banks to smile before returning to washing their clothes while little ones splashed around them.

At one point in the morning during a calm stretch of water, Kyle and I stopped to let some kids take turns jumping on the backs of our kayaks so we could paddle them around for a few minutes. They seemed to be in heaven, laughing with a pure joy I'm not sure I've ever felt myself. We must have looked like strangers from outer space in our colorful plastic ships, odd-looking helmets and poofy lifejackets, compared with these beings deeply connected to nature, clothed in old, dirt-infused fabric.

Unfortunately for Steve, he didn't show interest in joining in on the fun. He was more like a crotchety old man who kept his distance, not at all eager to engage with the clients, let alone the locals. I know you never know what people are going through, but c'mon, this was a social experience in a small, tightly knit group, and it was awkward when someone excluded themselves from the rest. Still, I will say he was very focused on his job and did it very well, as was evident that afternoon when two rafts flipped.

Again, this was not like the Ottawa, where it was just the clients in a raft on a warm sunny day. This was multi-day, so rafts were also carrying food and supplies and other essentials. Flipping could be a nightmare because sometimes those items came loose even if they were tied on properly. If a raft ended up upside down in a hydraulic (hole) and the raft got rattled in it (like I did in McCoy's), it could be violent enough that no amount of strapping would hold items in place. Then we were talking major clean-up, which just so happened to occur.

First, one raft full of clients flipped in a rapid, the name of which I could not remember. Steve and Kyle were on point, rescuing all six swimmers. Clients were not very good at holding onto their paddles, even though we drilled it into their brains to do so. Instinct would have you let go of anything that prevented you from using both arms to swim, so you couldn't blame them. In any case, what that meant for me was that I was off collecting paddles, which is awkward as fuck in a kayak.

It was all good in the end. Everyone made it to shore safe and intact while the guide jumped on the raft, flipped it over, got back in and paddled it to shore. These were lighter, six-man rafts as opposed to the rubber 12-man rafts of the Ottawa which made them much easier to deal with.

Liam gave the high sign for the next raft to go, which was the raft that was carrying most of the gear (the appropriately named 'gear raft'). This raft was a little bit different as it was rigged with an oaring system, so there was only one guide using oars secured to a steel frame on the raft. The oars were long and from what I could tell it looked complicated, but some guides preferred this system. Anyway, he somehow missed a stroke and slid into the hole sideways, which was an absolute fuck-up because it made it impossible to 'punch through'. In fact, if you wanted to flip, this would have been the perfect entry. And flip he did.

The interesting thing here was the raft guides on oar rigs were actually strapped into the boat. Eric had a waist strap so he wouldn't get launched into the air or thrown overboard in big rapids. On the bigger rafts I was used to, the guide would wedge their front foot under what was called a 'guide strap', an actual strap that goes across the back compartment of the raft that the guide could use to brace themselves. On the smaller rafts , the guide just wedged their foot between the floor and the seat in front of them. In other words, you needed some sort of way to prevent yourself from being tossed about and in an oar rig, this was the way.

When Eric hit the hole and immediately flipped, he had to keep his wits about him because he had to fucking reach down and pull his waist strap. I mean, who knew what was going on for him? All I knew was there were a couple of huge oars and gear and a lot to deal with, let alone setting yourself free of the raft and getting out from underneath it.

It was a hot mess. Still catching my breath from the last rescue, I was off again, chasing after gear. There were already two other rafts at the bottom, so thank God they could help with the clean-up, not to mention that clients loved getting in on the action, having to paddle hard to grab other people out of the water and basically help save the day.

When you fall out of a raft in moving water and have to try to save yourself by swimming in the direction we tell you, you can't help but be scared for your life. Some people are good at holding onto their paddle and figuring out which way to swim and can get themselves to safety. Others completely freeze and get all disoriented as to which way is upstream and downstream. Honestly, at that point, they couldn't find their way out of a wet paper bag. Either way, everyone was full of adrenaline and feeling very alive... and very happy to be alive.

As long as everyone was safe, it made for great synergy

around the campfire in the evenings, with lots of laughs and a growing sense of trust for the guides. From what I had gathered so far, all the guests were from a city, mostly in the U.S. There were a couple of lawyer friends and their wives, a doctor and her sister... Yeah, people looking for an escape from their high-stress jobs. I found it interesting that they chose adventure rafting, something I saw as polar opposite to their routine lives. From high-heels and suits to sandals and shorts. From asphalt to river. Yesterday I could tell they were uptight and resisting having to let go of control, but tonight I could see they were slightly more relaxed, shoulders not up to their ears, less tension in the face, more life behind their eyes.

For me personally, among a staff of all men, I felt particularly proud of myself for the part I played. Just like on the circuit, I had had to prove myself. Then again, maybe it had nothing to do with me being female. Maybe it was more that I had to prove myself to myself, that I was capable and strong and that it was okay to feel confident in my ability regardless of my limited experience. Maybe these guys were just a reflection of how I felt about myself. Where yesterday they reflected back my feelings of inadequacy, today they were reflecting back my adeptness and capabilities.

> **you're a queen**
> **and you've got what it takes!**
> **with all that style and grace**
> **and a big heart of gold**
> **simply be sure and 'know'**
> **you will accomplish your goals**

I lay in my tent later that evening listening to Seal's 'Kiss from a Rose' on my Walkman and dreaming of Liam lying next to me. It had become the theme song for this trip because I kept rewinding and listening to it over and over like ten times every night. I didn't bring it on the Annapurna because the batteries wouldn't have lasted in the cold, but I still managed to hum it to myself at night. That voice had become my personal lullaby. Add to that the bright sparkling stars in the Nepalese sky, and, well, the magic of life really had a way of shining in on your soul and making you feel whole.

Maybe this was how we were always supposed to feel. Maybe whole was normal, but we had become fragmented by fear and then fear had become our new normal.

Life was... confusing.

kali gandaki river day 3

. . .

I CAUGHT Liam watching me and smiling today on the river. I was feeling more relaxed and in the flow, and I think it must have shown, because when I paddled past his raft, he asked me to stop and hop in. We had hardly exchanged any words since the day I walked into the office and asked to join the trip. He was always multitasking and I never wanted to bother him. He obviously had a lot going on, so my admiration of him was from afar. This was exciting stuff.

"Tish, why not join us for a wee snack, aye?"

"Oh, okay!"

I was hell bent on playing it cool though I was sure if Fran had been here, she would have been laughing at the mere idea of it. I pulled my sprayskirt, leaned on the raft and hoisted myself up while Liam pulled my boat out of the water and rested it across the back of the raft.

The clients were all staring at me while I got out of my boat, and once I was seated, began a barrage of questions:

"How do you sit in that all day?"

"Where do your legs go?"

"Are you scared of dying?"

"How did you end up here?"

Smiling the whole time, Liam handed me a cup of juice while I fired back answers. When the clients were satisfied, they turned back to talking to one another, and Liam and I finally had a chance to talk.

"Was that a set-up?" I asked.

"Not at all, but I thoroughly enjoyed it."

"Well, now that you've learned all about me, what about you?"

"What about me?"

"How long have you been here? What's your deal?"

"Aye, well, I've been here for yonks."

"Huh?"

"Yonks. It means I've been here a long time. Came from Ireland some years back, but was only here briefly before traveling on to Bhutan, Tibet, and China. I was meant to continue on but I couldn't stop thinking about Nepal and had to come back. That was three years ago."

I loved his freckles.

"Hey, did you know this is the deepest canyon in the world?"

I don't know why I said that.

"Hadn't a baldy notion," he replied sarcastically.

"Huh?"

"Of course I knew that. Did you know it's a tributary of the Ganges, borders with Tibet, and is a popular trade route between Tibet and India?"

"Um, no."

Why on earth had I started a game of Nepalese facts with this guy?

"Alright lass, next rapid coming up shortly, so we're going to have to continue this conversation later."

He said we'd continue later. *Yessss!* I got back in my boat and he pushed me off the raft, launching me into the water.

Paddling to the next rapid, all I could think about was his mouth on mine.

Out of the five bigger rapids that day, I nailed three of them. Sure, 60% may not be the best percentage, but in the two I didn't nail and consequently flipped, I rolled back up both times. Kayaking was all in the recovery and I dare say my recoveries had improved immensely since Day 1. I was damn proud of myself. Even when I think back to the summer, I could tell I'd improved leaps and bounds on this trip. Maybe that was what happened when you averaged 15 km per day on the river. That was some good mileage.

Around the campfire, Liam taught us more about the river.

"This river is named after the Goddess Kali, who is considered a divine mother by the Hindus and worshiped here in Nepal as well as India. In Sanskrit, 'Kali' translates to 'she who is black' or 'she who is death'."

The guests looked at Liam with a sideways stare. He smirked, knowing all too well what they were thinking, having done this with guests on many trips prior.

"She is the goddess of time, creation, destruction and power. It's a lot, I know. And I know what you're thinking. Something along the lines of: Death? What might we be doing on a river of death?"

Everyone nodded and laughed, confirming his thoughts.

"Lads and lasses, there's nothing to fear. She destroys the evil in order to protect the innocent."

"So she's a superhero who kills the villains of the world?" I asked.

Our eyes met. And maybe it was the magic in the campfire, but it was like a meeting of the minds, if that made sense? The way he looked at me, I felt understood, like he knew me. That he knew my soul. I felt shy, having been seen so deeply, so quickly, and so unexpectedly. I immediately turned my gaze to the fire.

Liam continued:

"Aye Tish. Think of her as the changing aspect of nature, which in time brings things to life or death."

Thinking about how recently I'd walked alongside this river on the ascent of the Annapurna Circuit and was now paddling it intrigued me. I felt certain the Kali Gandaki River had been my spirit guide on this trip. From now on, I would keep her in my awareness.

Already I felt less alone.

kali gandaki river day 4

. . .

I WOKE UP FEELING ENERGIZED, despite a lack of sleep due to a new puncture in my Therm-a-Rest. After packing up my stuff, I helped put together a breakfast buffet of muesli, yogurt, fresh fruits, eggs, and toast. When the clients were done eating and I started cleaning up, Liam started packing the food.

"Mornin' lass, how you feeling today?"

"Hey, Liam. I'm feeling good. Somehow got a hole in my Therm-a-Rest, but it's all good. You?"

"Aye, always good on the river. I think I have a patch kit somewhere; I'll have a juke for it when we get to camp this afternoon."

"Okay, thanks."

I didn't know what 'juke' meant, but I didn't care. I only cared that he was talking to me, that my heart was in my stomach, and that it felt good to feel that feeling again. I was trying to think of something eloquent to say, eager for a conversation, but before I had a chance, he was called over to help load the rafts. Sigh. I really needed to be more forward, I decided, otherwise this trip would be over and I'd regret it.

The rapids today were a consistent Class III, which meant lots of fun waves with nothing of consequence that needed scouting first, like a big drop or a massive hole that would fuck you up if you didn't nail a specific line.

Later in the afternoon, we cruised around a bend on some light Class II and came upon a group of Nepalese all gathered by the shore around what looked like a dead body wrapped in white cloth. It was resting on what I presumed to be a funeral pyre. As we drifted past them and got a closer look, I swear to God I saw a small boy hammering down on the head of the dead body. *What the fuck?*

For the rest of the afternoon, I couldn't get that vulgar vision out of my mind. That night, as we ate around the campfire, Liam brought this cultural phenomenon to light:

"I know you don't have a baldy notion what we passed by today because I've been getting a lot of questions. So let's talk about Nepalese death, aye?"

We nodded our heads like good schoolchildren.

"Right. When death happens, the deceased is seen as a restless soul that has to be freed from its body in order to reach Heaven. It's a ritualistic process, but that ritual varies depending on city, caste, religion etc. Keep in mind I'm just sharing what I was told from a Nepalese guide a few years back, and I'm sure I'm missing many parts.

After death, Ganges water or other river water is sprinkled into the mouth of the dead before they are washed, anointed, and decorated. Then the body is wrapped in cloths of white cotton and yellow silk and put on the floor, which is coated with cow dung and weighted with a black stone or weapon so that the deceased will not rise again and the soul will not fly away before they are ritually prepared for the journey and can defend themselves against the evil spirits.

Then the corpse is carried out of the house. The procession is headed by the firstborn carrying the fire, followed by the corpse, feet first, and then relatives. Fun fact, women often don't join the procession or cremation. Can't remember why. Then it's carried to the cremation grounds along a special death path, then burned on a pyre made of wood, which is what we would have seen had we drifted by a little bit later than we did.

But now the part you've all been waiting for. The dead person is a sacrifice to the fire god Agni, who burns impurities and carries the spirit off to heaven in the smoke. Ritually speaking, cracking or smashing the skull is the most important moment of death. Once the skull has cracked or shattered, the thumb-sized individual soul can escape the body through a place along the hairline. It is said that the soul of bad people escapes through other bodily orifices, like the anus."

I looked at Kyle who was sitting next to me. "So it's basically a really big ordeal to die here..."

He looked back and laughed.

"That about sums it up, doesn't it? Though I sure can't imagine having to pound the skull of my father. That just... well... I don't know if I could... Could you?"

"Hell no. But if I was born and raised here and if it was a normal custom? Maybe I'd be desensitized."

I hesitated. I wasn't sure tradition would make it any less traumatic.

———

"Tish, lass, wait up a minute."

I was walking back to my tent, preparing myself for dreams of skull smashing, unable to get the vision out of my head since I witnessed it this afternoon when Liam stopped me. I was secretly hoping this would happen.

"That was quite the bedtime story, Liam, thanks for that."

"Yeah, about that, I wanted to show you something first. You fancy a dooter?"

...???

"Hmm, where I come from, that sounds a lot like something you wouldn't invite someone else to do with you."

"What's that?"

"Make doodoo."

"Naw, oh my lord, Tish, no. Dooter, it means a wee walk. I have something I want to show you."

"Oh, that makes better sense. Yeah, okay."

While I was doing my damnedest to act cool on the outside, my insides were doing somersaults.

With his headlamp leading the way, we followed the short beach area to its end, and climbed up some boulders out of sight of everyone else and up further still. Finally, we came to a flat rock on top of the boulders.

"Hang on a sec."

He laid out the blanket that was wrapped around his shoulders like a scarf, and signaled for me to lie down next to him. He turned his headlamp off and…

"Tada!" he said.

It was a beautiful sight indeed, the starry sky its own theatrical event. But I was so nervous that I was shaking. So much so that it was obvious.

"You okay, lass?"

"Yep, yep, just a bit chilly."

I couldn't have him know how nervous I was to be alone with him. That would be completely uncool and I was desperate not to have yet another guy recoil like Jerry did. I wasn't about to shy away from him, but I also wasn't about to be forthright.

"Here, get closer."

Liam pulled me close to him, my head now resting on his arm.

"Is that better?"

"Um, yes, thanks."

Fuck, fuck, fuck, fuck, now what? We lay there, staring at the stars while my mind ran wild. Should I do something? Do I need to make the first move?

"So Tish, tell me about the Ottawa River…"

Thank God he interrupted my pathetic inner dialogue and led the way. As conversation started, the night began. We talked for a solid hour, getting to know one another. He was witty in his Irish humor. After a while I stopped shaking, and as more time passed, I felt more and more comfortable, finally relaxing into this intimate moment. I was having fun and feeling ready for more. He must have sensed it, because he hoisted himself up on his elbow to face me, put his other arm around me, and leaned in…

I did not shy away, meeting my lips with his, his soft beard brushing against my chin and cheeks as our tongues danced effortlessly together. It felt beautifully natural. My fears melted away with the sensuality of our intertwining energies. He pulled me on top of him, then rolled us over so that I was on my back. He slipped his hand under my shirt, mine under his… feeling, caressing, caring…

He whispered in my ear before licking it and moving onto my neck.

"Tish, lass, what do you say we take this somewhere a little bit more comfortable?"

"Yeah, um, yes… yes."

While one part of me worried the magic of the moment would be ruined as soon as we moved, the other part of me couldn't imagine doing anything more on the hard slab of rock. Eventually we got up, crawled back down the boulders and headed back to the beach where we were camped. Glad to be wrong, the anticipation of what was to come only heightened our vibe, and by the time we snuck into his tent, we were hungry for more. I was already gushing with excitement when he slipped his fingers in me.

"Tish, oh my God, you're so wet!"

I didn't know if that was something I should be embarrassed about, whether it was abnormal or not, but I didn't care. I just wanted him in me.

"Thank you?" I said, and we both started laughing.

I reached down and pulled his cock out of his pants. He was harder than that rock we'd been lying on, but this was something I could comfortably rest on. He slid into me easily and moaned at the first point of entry. Finally!

He was a good fit, just the right length, just the right width to fill me up. My legs spread wide, welcoming him to go deep, I met his rhythm, moving my hips as he pulled in and out. He knew how to move, that much was certain. He was just as confident with me as he was with the river.

Fuck. I was already close to coming. There was only so much we could do, position wise, in this epically small tent, so I rolled him over onto his back so that I could be on top, control the timing and slow it down… to hold out for just a little bit longer.

"Mmm, Tish, you are a badass."

Did he really just call me that? Was I a badass? The idea that he thought I was made me ride him harder, sinking into him deeper. I arched my back, ecstasy igniting within me, within both of us. Building, building, building… until together we…

"MMMMMMmmmmmooohhhh."

Oh. My. God. I WAS a badass!

Afterwards, we lay there, nestled into each other, fully satisfied. Never before had I come at the same time as someone else. Well, Dusty had been the only guy who'd given me the opportunity, and for whatever reason, we never synced up quite like this.

"By the way, Tish, I have to be honest," Liam said as we were still catching our breath, "I *did* find that patch kit, but I didn't tell you because I had no intention of you needing to use it tonight."

I looked over at him and smiled.

"I was hoping that would be the case."

"Did you really?"

"Um, yeah, hot Irish guy telling funeral pyre stories at the campfire? Sexy as fuck."

kali gandaki river day 5 - travel light

. . .

I SNUCK out his tent at dawn, before anyone was up. I still could not believe what had happened. I will say this much: we didn't get much sleep, and spent much of the night rolling around together, talking, laughing, exploring each other's bodies. I surprised myself. I was open, relaxed, confident, the opposite of what I usually felt in the company of men I liked. It felt amazing, like the night had cracked open some dark mysterious vault within me, shining its light on whatever I thought I needed to hide.

Now I'd seen there *was* nothing to hide, at least not in the right company.

> the sunrise is yours
> the sunset is too
> believe in your Self
> and your light will always shine through

I was in a daze packing up my stuff and helping out, relieved to get on the river where I could collect my thoughts and get my head in the game for the one big rapid today. It was a picturesque morning in Nepal. The air crisp, the sun bright, the sky infinite.

Walk in the Dark was a long Class IV rapid, and the biggest rapid since Little Brother and Big Brother on Day 1. The guides were scouting the rapid from shore, so they had a perfect viewing point as I entered. I liked that they were there to watch, and I could hear them all cheering for me as I skillfully maneuvered my way down. I had given myself some solid landmarks to gauge where I wanted to be at the more crucial points. I kept my focus and held my line, arriving at the bottom in perfect alignment with the river.

It was a nice change—especially since Liam was one of them— to have onlookers cheering on my success instead of cheering on my beatdown like at McCoy's, an embarrassing experience forever etched in my brain.

From that point on, it was Class II all the way, and aside from accidentally ramming into a dead, bloated cow floating in an eddy, everything was a breeze to the take-out where yet another huge sense of accomplishment awaited.

Life was awesome!

———

The drive back to Pokhara was heartwarming, nestled comfortably among the gear on top of the bus with Liam. I was extremely proud of myself for having made it through all the twists and turns of this particular journey, especially now that I'd emerged on the other side more confident than ever. And I wasn't just talking about my river skills.

"Where are you off to next, Tish?" Liam asked, his arm around me, both of us half-asleep, the bus no longer life-threatening.

"Hmm, good question." I replied. "Any suggestions?"

While I wanted to cling to the idea of spending more time with him now that we'd had that beautiful night together, I knew in my heart it could not extend any further and that it would be better to let it go as quickly as it came. He would soon be off on another trip, and I would be going elsewhere too.

"Yeah, I've got some ideas for you, lass. Why don't we talk about it over dinner, and one more night together?"

I nodded in agreement. "That sounds perfect."

His intentions were clear: one more night. Perhaps this was how he played his game. For a split second, I wanted to grasp onto the idea that I was just another of his river conquests, but seeing how upset it was already making me, I decided against it. Besides, so what if I was?

I relaxed. There was something peaceful about our connection. Maybe it was because I wasn't future-tripping about being with him, or whether he'd like me if he *really* got to know me. There was something truly special about living in the moment and enjoying all it had to offer. No expectations. No defining what it meant. Just the freedom of connection.

That night, we reveled in it one last time.

> **'SHHH' says my big heart**
> **you're fine my sweetheart**
> **just let your thoughts clear**
> **there's simply nothing to fear**
> **so surrender to LOVE**
> **and know that it's always here**

The next morning as he stood in the doorway, neither of us asked to exchange contact info. In fact, the only thing we did exchange was a bow and a Namaste before he turned, walked out of my room at Hotel Nirvana and was gone.

I flopped onto my bed, closed my eyes, and tapped into my dreamy imaginings of the previous evening's festivities, rolling around in them for as long as I could. What a divine way to end this trip! The thrill of my adventures in Nepal had only strengthened my desire for more.

And thanks to Liam, I had a plan for my next destination.

But first I would have to break the news to my parents.

part iii

twenty-nine

. . .

April 1998

"YOU'RE DOING WHAT?"

I had told my parents I was going traveling for a year. Knowing how hard this would be on them, I made an intention to *not* take their reactions personally. Instead, I focused solely on the fact that they were my parents and I loved them.

> **it's a glorious choice**
> **to use your great voice**
> **so be clear on the matter**
> **use love to break old patterns**
> **it takes practice and strength**
> **but I know you've got what it takes**
> **so go forth with your mind**
> **and always be kind!**

This time around my father's disapproving glances were extra special. I could tell by the way his eyes darted across the room that his concern was all jumbled up with confusion as to how his daughter, after all he had invested in her upbringing, had chosen to become a dirty bum.

"Jesus Christ, my daughter's a vagabond."

I glanced down at my outfit: Chaco River sandals, cut-off jean shorts, and my favorite t-shirt from when I bungee-jumped 82 meters off the Zambezi Bridge. I still didn't see what the problem was. Maybe I should get dreadlocks, pierce my nose, start wearing patchouli oil and get a sleeve tattoo... Then we would really see if this, me, was so bad.

"Tish, when are you going to stop fooling around and join the real world?"

He just couldn't help himself. This must have been building up since the minute I'd walked through the door. Growing up, I'd learned his pattern: he'd withhold his opinion so as not to offend, usually saying something like 'don't get *me* involved', but he was a man of strong opinions, and in the end those thoughts and opinions would build silently, one on top of the other until, all of a sudden... *bleughhh!* He would purge a huge cluster of harsh words. He got it 'out of his system' as my mom liked to say, and then he was done. He felt better and simply moved on in a wonderfully new mood, unaware of the fact that he'd left a trail of stink bombs in his wake.

Come to think of it, this was where I got my outbursts from! Except I had also been raised to be well-mannered, which also explained my feelings of guilt and shame.

"Don't worry, Dad. I'll stop when I'm 29."

At 25, my hope was to present him with the idea that I'd 'join the real world' before I turned 30 to save him some stress on the matter, while earning me a few years of peace from his badgering disdain. It did. He bit into it with relief, and I could feel the tension dissipating, the dark cloud above his head lifting. Poor guy. He had no idea I was completely bullshitting him.

Twenty-nine was just a number I'd blurted out so that he would stop bothering me. Lying, fabricating, vague responses... that was the kind of thing you did when you needed to get people off your back. I didn't feel bad for it, either. Why should I? Nobody had the right to deter me from my path regardless of who or what that path was.

That was love, wasn't it? Well, self-love, anyway. Maybe it wasn't the perfect approach, but it was the best I could do at the time. And in my opinion, it was a success because this time I didn't get angry, this time I didn't let him disturb my peace. I played his game while still playing mine, and that was a smart move.

> **reflect on your past**
> **to see what you've learned**
> **acknowledge what's gone**
> **without gripping on**
> **instead…**
> **come back to the now**
> **feel the love…**
> **and know it's all around**

With nothing left to say, I went to my room and listened to my Alanis Morissette CD while enthusiastically packing for the next adventure.

RF: "Wow! You're particularly excited for a full year of not knowing what's going to unfold."

Me: "I am."

RF: "This is all because of Liam's influence. What makes you think it's going to be *all* that?"

Me: "It's just a feeling I have. I'm ready to dive deeper into the flow."

RF: "You're becoming quite the existentialist."

Me: "Hey, try to be happy for me."

RF: "I am. I liked Liam. His red hair, anyway."

Me: "Of course you did."

There was a quiet knock on the door.

"Tish? Can I come in?"

It was my mom.

"Yes, of course."

Mom entered and closed the door behind her. She sat on my bed.

"What's up?" I asked innocently.

"You know our concern only comes from the fact that we just want what's best for you…"

I took a deep breath, promising myself to hear her out without getting defensive.

"…and I know your father blurts things out in the worst way possible, but it's only because he loves you and worries about you…"

"Hmmm," I said calmly. "I get that, I do. But you know, mom, worry isn't love."

"Well, of course, it is, dear. I worry about you because I love you and I don't want anything to happen to you."

"But how is worry love? Worry is fear, and fear isn't love."

We sat in silence for a few minutes. I think she was confused by what I had said. Parents think it's good that they worry because it means they care, but from my observation it's terribly misguided.

"Worry only gives *you* migraines, Mom. It doesn't provide *me* with safety. It doesn't do anything except hurt *you*. And, actually, it hurts me to know you're hurting, and I don't want to carry that with me while I'm traveling! How can it be love if it hurts? It would be better if you… if you *both* could find a way to trust me, and trust my path. You know I'm going to do what I want anyway, so why spend so much time resisting it? I love you, and I wish you could be on my side…"

After some more silence, she finally spoke.

"Well, you certainly are learning a lot about life, aren't you?"

"*Thank* you!"

We hugged it out, and it felt good to be heard and possibly even understood. As she was leaving, she turned and added, "I love you, Tish, and I'm proud of you," then closed the door behind her.

I feel a glimmer of hope
as I give way to the flow
and as it unfolds
it becomes clear as day
love will always be with me
to brighten my way.

———

RF: "Bravo! Bravo!"
　　Me (bowing): "Why thank you, my friend."
　　It seemed things were aligning on all sides.

a real date

· · ·

January 1999

"TEEESH!!! WHEN AN ITALIAN MAN TAKES YOU TO DINNER..."

His hands were waving in the air, his eyebrows raised up high on his dark crinkled forehead, eyes passionately disturbed, voice loud, full of frustration at my attempt to split the bill with him.

We were sitting at a table outside under the starry sky of Jinja, Uganda, fenced in with string lights and tiki lamps, the single candle on our table flickering in the light breeze lighting up the expressiveness of his dark brown eyes.

"Okay, okay! I'm sorry, I'm sorry!" I interrupted. I was just trying to be polite. I'm Canadian! And all backpackers only pay their share. But in his mind, I had insulted him.

"Aye yai yai, Teeesh!"

He was shaking his head now, his hands pressed up against either side of his temples in dismay. He was being very dramatic in my opinion, but that was the Italian way.

"I want to take you to eat at this nice place! I want to share nice meal with you, this nice place. You. And me. I PAY! I'M ITALIAN!"

Again with the hands.

He moved here only three months ago and didn't have a lick

of English under his belt, yet here he was, clearly translating his thoughts into words.

> the jaws of love are wide open
> make your move, don't be shy!
> spring forth into action
> a heart full of passion can't lie.

Stefano. My Italian lover.

a meeting at the market

. . .

OUR MUTUAL FRIEND Leonardo introduced us at Explorers Bar several evenings ago. This was the main watering hole where the raft guides and clients got drunk and sloppy every night. I was instantly drawn to him, partly because he wasn't drunk or sloppy, but mostly because of his beautifully thick accent and the way he proudly introduced himself.

"Ah, hallo Teesh. I *am* Stefano."

That, and those deep, dark, warmly-lit eyes. I was desperate to talk to him, but it was too loud to strike up a real conversation, and since I wasn't up for awkward small talk, I wandered to the other side of the bar and stared at him from afar, undressing him with my eyes like a creepy stalker.

A few days later, I ran into him serendipitously at the market in Jinja and wasted no time taking advantage of this unexpected opportunity. I know, I know, you're thinking that that doesn't at all sound like the normal 'me,' but I'd been traveling for the last eight months and had learned a great many things along the way, one of them being that there was no point wasting time in going after what you wanted, including men.

That was the thrill of traveling solo. With no obligations, routines, or attachments, you become quite adept at acting on all of those sudden urges. It's as easy as: *Do I want to do this?* If it's a yes, it's a go. If it's a no, it's no big deal. There's no need to compromise or sacrifice your own happiness in order to accommodate other people's needs.

And let me tell you, it's incredibly satisfying. Liberation at its finest, because those urges were mine and all mine, and they had taken me to many places and given me many crazy (though not always the good kind of crazy) experiences.

First, I went heli-boating in New Zealand, which was where you take a helicopter to the put-in, boats and gear hanging from the helicopter in a large mesh net. I went with a bunch of adventurous Germans on the most beautifully remote rivers.

Then, I went on a walkabout and tried surfing in Australia (love the Aussies), rock-climbing in Thailand (I sucked, and sucked worse at hooking up with rock-climbing men), smoked opium and rode an elephant in Cambodia, did more kayaking in Costa Rica (not a fan of their 'gringo tax') where I met Leonardo, who also told me all about his upcoming rafting job in Uganda.

When I got to Ecuador, things took a turn for the worse. Oh man, this next bit is really hard to say. Tears are welling up in my eyes at the thought of it, so I'm just going to come out with it.

Red Fran was *stolen*.

Ugh. I'm still so angry about it I have murder on my mind. And that happened at the *end* of an already-harrowing experience. It's still painful to talk about in detail, but the gist of it was this:

I went on an overnight kayaking trip on the Rio Hollin with some random kayakers I met at the hotel we were staying at in Tena. During the night, while we were camped out, it unexpectedly poured rain and there was a flash flood. The next morning, the river had risen three feet, which is a lot. The river was brown, moving incredibly fast with tree branches and logs floating by while we watched from shore, wondering what to do. Because we didn't want to wait for it to pass (who knew how long that would be?) and because we didn't bring enough supplies for more than the night, we stupidly put on the river.

An hour in, I got sucked into a huge hole, swam, lost my boat, but was thankfully rescued by one of the guys and managed to get to shore. We re-grouped, again wondering what to do while the water continued to rise and rise. When a piranha jumped out of the water, we freaked and decided it was best not to go any further. Not that I could go anywhere without a boat. We climbed a cliff to a flat area, huddled together and camped out for another night.

The next day, everyone was cold, hungry, and anxious to leave. One of the guys, Andrew, waited it out with me while the others planned to get to the take-out and have us rescued. But the water was still dangerously high, and as I would find out later, they had gone on to have their own harrowing experience. In the meantime, Andrew and I were lost in the jungle for three days with nothing but two mangoes and a bottle of rum.

On the third day, because the flood had passed and the river was once again do-able, we rigged up his kayak for me to hang onto the back, and just as we were about to leave shore we saw two kayakers upstream, paddling towards us. Rescuers! It was a godsend that we happened to be at the river's edge at the exact moment they were about to paddle by, otherwise they would never have found us. The rescuers said that some others were hiking in, but we were to meet up further downstream on the other side of the river. Off we went to this random spot, with Andrew and the other two guys leaving me there alone to wait for my rescuers while they paddled to the take-out.

After an hour, I got impatient and began hiking up, hoping to meet them along the way. It was brutally hard in every which way. Would I meet them? Would I survive? Would I be stuck in the jungle at night by myself? I was scared, I was angry, I was tired. I cried a lot. At one point, I almost gave up until I saw a chicken and realized that there must be a farm or something nearby. With newfound optimism, I found a trail and followed it, which led me to an Ecuadorian family and their 'farm' in the jungle. They were ultra shocked at my magical appearance. When I asked 'camino?' they simply pointed.

I followed the only trail for a couple more hours, wondering if I was on the right path. Then, I heard my name. Or was I delusional? I heard my name again, and yelled back. They'd found me! The rescuers who had hiked in had gone too far down the river and were on their way back, hoping to find me along the way. It was yet another miracle.

I was met with hugs, and some shoes and clothes that they had gotten from my room. I guzzled water, but with no daylight to spare we continued on our way for another four hours. We made it to the main road just before dusk, met the taxi, and finally, after four days on that damn river, I was back at the hotel.

I had survived the ordeal, only to go back to my room and find a bunch of my stuff gone. Nobody knew what had happened from the time they left my room to the time we returned. Luckily, I had hidden my passport and money behind the light fixture, but my camera and a few other items were gone...

Including Red Fran.

It was heartbreaking. I was already utterly exhausted, sad, relieved, and every other emotion, but to lose Red Fran, my constant companion? It felt like the world was crumbling beneath me. And what about her? I couldn't even imagine what she was going through, having been kidnapped.

What could I do about it?

Absolutely nothing.

I had originally planned on spending more time in Ecuador, but after such an ordeal, I was completely done with this place. It might have made more sense to continue traveling South America, but Leonardo had planted the seed of Uganda and I couldn't stop thinking about it. I had four months left in my one-year plan, and decided to finish it there. It was an easy yes, even though without Fran I felt painfully alone. But I had no choice except to let go.

it's good to stand alone
feel the comfort on your own
with two feet keeping you grounded
it's safe to let go
and let your mind unwind
because your soul already knows

My mom said I was a glutton for punishment, but was supportive nonetheless. I had begun calling her every other week because I missed her and knew she'd always be anxious to hear from me. I didn't want her to worry more than she already was, but truthfully it was good to hear her loving voice. My dad chimed in on occasion, but letter writing had always been a much better form of communication for us. Whenever I had an address of a hostel I was staying at, I'd always let him know and he'd always, without fail, send me a letter. By sending letters, we could take time carefully selecting our words. It also protected me from his spontaneous outbursts of negativity towards my life choices, and that was good enough reason for me to keep going with this method. I think he liked it too. It was our safe zone.

Still, I was more particular with what I shared with them and they no longer tried to sway me this way or that. All in all, we were more successful in our efforts towards each other.

———

Anyway, back to the market in Jinja:

"Oh! Stefano! What... what are you doing here?"

"Ah, Teesh! Do I say that right? I'm sorry... my Engleesh..."

"Teesh is perfect," I replied.

We stood in silence for a moment, though it wasn't awkward —more like that comfortable silence with a bunch of friends after getting high, until I caved and broke the silence.

"Hey, Stefano, I want to get to know you."

I could tell from his smile that he knew I was into him. He

lingered in the satisfaction of it, which made me feel embarrassed. I probably blushed. Was I about to be rejected?

"Ah, I am looking for shorts. You would to help me?"

Wow, that was an instantaneous manifestation. Whew! And off we went into the clothing area of the market. It was nothing fancy, just the dirt ground with a bunch of tables protected under old and torn tarps. Most structures I had witnessed in the rural towns in Africa were makeshift. *Use what you can find and make it work.* And they did. But when it started to downpour all of a sudden out of a clear blue sky, we learned that nothing was rainproof, as water droplets passed through the holes in the tarps, turning the dirt to mud and splashing onto our feet. Stefano grabbed my hand and pulled me to take cover under one of the more semi-dry stalls.

So there we were. Nestled together under a tarp, laughing, enjoying the spontaneity of life.

Damn, he's attractive, I thought to myself, even though he wasn't in the slightest the typical guy I'd be attracted to, which made him all the more intriguing. I tended towards the tall and muscular 'dudes,' whereas Stefano was of average height and size. He was strong, I supposed, but he didn't necessarily look fit, especially when compared to the local Ugandan raft guides who were naturally lean, bulging with muscles and statuesque in height. He had this thick silver necklace and bracelet, which marked him an Italian *gino,* but at least he didn't have greased-back hair and designer clothes so, you know, that was good. His black hair was short and thick, as was his short beard, likely the growth from only a day or two. I generally liked my men less… hairy. He was definitely not that, especially not with that chest hair curling up and out of the collar of his t-shirt. But strangely, none of it mattered. There was something about him that was more powerful than my prejudices.

The rain stopped as abruptly as it started, and in those brief minutes, I found myself more attracted to him than I'd ever been attracted to anyone. He smiled at me and I could feel the love in his eyes.

"Come. We look at shorts?"

The lady behind the table in the stall where we had taken cover smiled at him and said, "Go! Look!"

She pointed to the table where there were multiple piles of shorts in all sizes and varieties.

Stefano rummaged through the piles, pulling out shorts as he went along, holding them up for me to see and then putting them on over his shorts.

"Teesh, what do you think?"

I adored how comfortable he was trying on shorts in front of me and asking for my input. Look at us, already shopping together!

take one

. . .

OVER THE COURSE of the week, we saw each other almost every day. It wasn't hard, given the quaintness of the rafting and kayaking community. We were all centrally located near the top of Bujagali Falls, the first rapid. This was also the location of the only bar, where we'd met, and where I was camping a mere 30 feet away at Eden Roc campground.

Stefano lived five or six kilometers away at the property of the rafting company where he worked, and it was easy to taxi back and forth via *boda boda* (that is to say, a local man on a moped). It was the predominant mode of transport in this area, and a way for many men to make their living.

I hadn't expected to be so smitten with anyone while on this trip, especially while still recovering from the loss of Red Fran, but the force was too strong to deny and I could not ignore such a good-feeling impulse. Even as I stood there watching him flail about in frustration when I tried splitting the bill, in the midst of the drama, all I saw was a passionate Italian who cared deeply to fulfill his role as 'man'.

Romantic, right?

So, that's how we came to be there. A Canadian and an Italian at a Mediterranean restaurant in Uganda, trying to get life right.

He paid the bill obviously and I felt a bit shitty for having killed what could've been a very sweet moment. It wasn't often I'd been asked out on an actual date. Looking back, maybe that was because I simply didn't know how to accept it. That's how adept I had become at rejection, or at least the expectation of it. Sad, I know.

I hopped on the back of the motorcycle he had borrowed from a friend for this special evening, and off we rode into the night, back to his place where he shared a room with Leonardo.

Their third buddy, Pablo from Costa Rica, was the video boater. They were quite the threesome: good-hearted, good-natured, good vibes. Some guys could be real dicks, especially when they're drunk and full of bravado (ego), but these were the kind who I knew would have my back. The other two spoke English quite well, so it was Stefano who had to work the hardest to understand the conversation.

"So you really didn't speak any English before you came here?" I asked while we lay on the mattress on the floor of Pablo's single room. (Yep, Pablo had given us his room so that we could be alone together. A bro code, I'm sure.)

"No English, Teesh. I just learn here from rafting."

"Like from being a raft guide?"

"YES, Teesh. I learn 'paddle on left, stop, paddle back...' You know, words to direct. Then I learn more words."

"But like, you speak really well for only a few months."

"I am smart man, Teesh!" he said proudly, as he pulled my shirt over my head.

Was it weird to be in Pablo's room, knowing that he and Leonardo knew what we were up to? Was this the fuck room? Did they take turns in here? How many women had they had on this mattress? Yikes. I needed to change my train of thought so I didn't kill the mood.

Also, I should clarify that while I was now much more forthright in approaching men, and while I had had a few fun nights during my travels, I was also very picky. In other words, I hadn't turned into some sex-craving sleazemonger. No, even from as far back as Frank in Zimbabwe, I had learned that sex was extremely unfulfilling when it lacked sensuality, so the men I allowed into my bed had been few and far between. Let me think. Hmm... the last guy I'd had was—oh right—Mark in New Zealand. And come to think of it, Liam was still on the top of my satisfaction list, leaving a standard that apparently was hard to live up to.

Anyway, I thought for sure Stefano would meet those standards. He had slept in my tent with me the other night, and while we had kept it above the belt, his kisses were delightfully juicy, and not in the sloppy kind of way. Unlike other guys who were just so boringly eager to get their cocks out, it felt like Stefano was actually *into* me.

"Teesh, come to me... I am to kiss you all over."

And he did. He gave wholeheartedly without trying to make it more than it was. He loved on me. Of course, this took me by surprise, these feelings that were being awakened within me. I was *into* it but didn't know what to *do* with it.

It was clear that sex was on the agenda tonight, though, and I desperately hoped my heart was ready, fully expecting our intertwining to be off-the-charts hot. But it was not. Not even a little bit.

What happened? How could I have been so off-base? Aren't Italians supposed to be incredible lovers? Unlike the sweet, sensual kisses from the other night, he was jack hammering me like... what the fuck? *Pound, pound, pound.* For some reason unknown to me, I didn't want to hurt his feelings, so I moaned and pretended to like it. But honestly? It was horribly wrong. Why was I protecting him from the truth? God only knows. Although to be fair, in the moment, I had just been trying to figure out what was going on and wondering if it was going to get better. Frankly, I just didn't know what to do! I was shocked and appalled. This man had destroyed the passionate fantasy I had created of us in my mind.

After he came, and after I pretended to come, we lay on the mattress, staring above, into the darkness. My heart fell flat.

Stefano. My Italian lover?

―――――

While Stefano slept, I thought about Red Fran, missing her company. Even though we argued a lot and had our differences, we had gone through so many adventures together and I wished I could talk to her now, or at least listen to her mock me for thinking this could be more than random sex. She may not have always had it right, but she didn't always have it wrong, either. I wondered where she was, if she was happy, if she was with someone who was enjoying all the annoyances that she brought to the table. I just couldn't bear the thought of her being in the hands of someone else.

I had to remind myself there was nothing I could do except let her go. It was the only way to lighten my load.

The next morning Pablo and Leonardo were all smiles as we approached the pavilion for breakfast.

"Chichileo!" they hollered.

"Chichi what?" I asked Stefano.

"Ah, chichileo, Teesh. Don't worry. Is what we always say. Erm, like, hello, but in our way."

I sat down at the table with them while Stefano got us some coffee from the communal kitchen.

"Did you have a good night?" Pablo was smirking and winking, being way too obvious.

I felt like I was at the cafeteria at lunch in grade school getting pestered by an annoying boy. At least, I imagined that's what it would've been like, based on the high school rom coms I loved watching. I went to a private girls' school, remember, so I never had the pleasure of... *this*.

Leonardo smiled sympathetically from across the table before turning back to his eggs and letting me be. The yin to Pablo's yang. I smiled quietly back, grateful.

"Here, for you. Coffee."

Stefano placed the cup down in front of me, then put his arm around me and planted a kiss on my cheek. He was proud to show me off in front of his friends, and my heart began to sing for him once again. He really was so sweet.

"So you guys have a big day today?"

I was referring to a raft trip, which, due to high tourism, was on the daily.

"Yes, yes," Leonardo replied, "I think we have 30 people today?"

"Ah yes, Teesh, so I must eat quickly. Do you want something from the chicken?"

"Excuse me, what?"

"To eat. You would to eat? I would go to the chicken."

I had to pause and translate.

"Oh, you mean kitchen!"

Too cute.

"Yes, Teesh, yes, what I said?"

"KITchen not CHIcken. Chicken is the bird! You know. *Bawk! Bawk!*" I clucked, flapping my arms.

"Ah yes, yes. Wait, what?"

"KITchen."

"Keetchen. KEETchen. Aye yai yai!"

By this point, we were all laughing hysterically. For Leonardo and Pablo, English was their second language so they could absolutely relate. For me, it was a moment of appreciation, because even though English was my native tongue, I understood all too well what it was like trying to communicate in a foreign language or culture. Taiwan came to mind. I felt the soft spot for Stefano rise up again in my heart, and decided that maybe last night's unfortunate less-than-mind-blowing sex was an isolated incident.

giving it another go

· · ·

I HAD PROMISED I'd try to meet up with their raft trip, but by the time I got home to my tent, got ready, and finally threw my boat over my shoulder to walk down to the put-in, I could see from my epic view of the river a few hundred feet away, their red and black rafts floating towards the first rapid. By the time I hiked down and got in the water, I knew they would be long gone and I just wasn't up for the chase. Instead, I caught up with Don and Scott, two guys staying at my campground, who were also gearing up for a paddle, and asked to join them.

We stopped just outside our campsite on the main road to organize our shuttle. This meant choosing three of the seven or eight guys on boda bodas to pick us up at the takeout.

Before we go any further, some things to know about the Nile River... At 6650km, it is the longest river in the world, though some would argue the Amazon is the longest. Lake Victoria is considered the source of the Nile, and it flows northward, spanning 11 countries. It has two main tributaries: the White Nile and the Blue Nile. The section of the White Nile in Uganda that goes from Lake Victoria and all the way up to Lake Albert, the section I was on, also goes by the Victoria Nile.

This river was probably the most intimidating water I'd seen to date. Over the last few years, Uganda had become a popular kayaking destination, due in part to a video that a couple of guys from South Africa made. Watching these guys in their kayaks made it look seriously insane, like they were the biggest dare-devils taking on the most terrifying of rivers, a river so big they looked like little tadpoles about to be swallowed by a whale. The volume in this deep, wide stretch of river was tremendous, which means it has holes at least five times the size of Phil's Hole on the Ottawa. It was extremely intimidating, to say the least. However, it also showed some really fun waves and other sections of the river that seemed manageable. When Leonardo showed me the video in Costa Rica, and I saw these guys on the backs of boda bodas with their kayaks, the infamous red Bujagali mud on their clothes which stains everything an orange tinge, and the monkeys, wildlife, the sunsets and nightlife, well, I knew I had to go.

Although this section called the Silverback was short and fun, I still found the massive volume of water intimidating. I acted nonchalant on the outside, but the inner me was still dealing with PTSD from the traumatic time in Ecuador. One might wonder why I didn't quit kayaking after that trip, but I needed to get back up on that horse, right? I'm happy to report I'd successfully paddled this two-mile section of the river every day for the last two weeks—and had become comfortably familiar with it.

The thing with big water is that it's hard to gauge your surroundings, like being lost at sea. The best time to get perspective is when you reach the top of a wave. That's when you can see where you're at comparative to shore and what part of the rapid you're in. That's also when you have to decide quickly what strokes you need to put in before you plummet down the backside of the wave.

Here, you'd start at Ribcage, a Class IV, aptly named for its dangerous tree roots in the middle of the current. The week before

I had arrived, a Frenchman had drowned on this rapid. Nobody knows what happened except that he disappeared midway down and never popped up. Rumor had it a local man found his body further downstream and was keeping it, wanting money in exchange. Whether this was true, I did not know.

> **look at the view**
> **breathe in**
> **you've got what it takes**
> **all you need is to be brave**
> **forget the past**
> **and see life anew**

Next was Bujagali Falls, which dropped over a bedrock ledge. For me, this was pretty chill. Luckily, I had my big water Ottawa River background which boosted my confidence when I realized that Don and Scott were less used to big water and more accustomed to creeks and steep rivers. I could see the nervousness in Don's eyes as I watched him from the bottom of Bujagali Falls when he came flying down.

I tended to believe that all guy kayakers would be better than me. I don't know where this belief came from; maybe because most of the guys I knew back on the Ottawa were already experienced boaters. Same with Nepal. Noticing that I was actually ahead of the curve now compared with a number of the guys enabled me to shake off what was left of my nerves. Finally, I wasn't the worst paddler in the group! I don't say that in any derogatory way. It had nothing to do with them and everything to do with the shift in my mindset. On the one hand, I had benefited from being the least experienced paddler because it forced me to be constantly outside my comfort zone, always pushing my limits. On the other hand, it wasn't always fun being the weakest link in the chain.

God, I remember this one time Dusty and I were scouting

Garvin's Chute on the middle channel of the Ottawa. He was pointing out the line and I asked, "What happens if you go there?" pointing to outside the line.

Him: "You don't go there."

Me: "Yeah, but what if I do?"

Him: "You just don't go there!"

Me: "Yeah but…"

Him: "YOU'LL DIE, TISH! IF YOU GO THERE, YOU'LL DIE!"

Jesus fuck. Needless to say, from that point on, I've always been scared of not hitting my line. I wonder if that's affected me in other areas of my life too—the need to be perfect —because if I wasn't, bad things would happen. Hmm, doesn't leave any room at all for error, now does it? That's the difference between men and women: women think of consequences; men just move full steam ahead, never wondering what will happen if things go wrong. Maybe that's why we have a longer life span.

Now the tables had turned and I was getting my first taste of what it's like to lead. The next rapid, called 50/50, was a big wave train (series of successive waves). I spent less time thinking about getting through it and more time looking back to make sure my boys were on point. It was such a good feeling to know that, if they could do this, I could definitely do it! From then on, I was more relaxed, which always made life more fun.

Next up, Total Gunga, a much larger wave train with a monster wave lurking somewhere in the middle called G-Spot. You never knew if it was going to be green or surging or what you'd get when you hit it. Then on to Surf City, another wave train, before reaching the horizon line of Silverback, a series of even bigger waves that, once through, completed the rollercoaster ride.

But wait, we're not done yet!

The take-out was at the eddy on river right where we went up the hill on the dirt path to meet our boda bodas. I mean, this was seriously just as much fun as running the river. Imagine sitting on the back of a moped, resting your kayak on your lap between you and the driver and trying to hold it in place while your driver whizzes back along mud tracks through the villages. It was so awesome! That is, unless your moped runs out of gas halfway back.

"Not to worry, sista!" Freddy, my driver, said as he proceeded to open the gas tank, cover it with his mouth and blow air into it, while I sat on the back feeling like we were for sure stranded and the other guys would have no idea because they were already too far ahead to notice.

Freddy tried to start the engine but it didn't work, so again he uncapped the gas tank and began blowing into it again. *I guess I could just start walking.* It would have taken a while, and I probably would have had a group of little kids following along, wanting to hold my paddle. I didn't mind the stares and curiosity coming from the locals as I passed by their huts because that happened regardless of whether I was on foot, by *matatu* (small van), or boda boda.

Just as I was about to get off, Freddy started up the motor and we were driving back to the campground. I was shocked we made it back without running out of gas again, but I would come to learn this was the norm, and that these guys knew enough to get the job done.

"Tish, where'd you go? We thought we lost you," Don said, welcoming me back to the campsite where he and Scott were already chilling in the pavilion with a beer.

"Ran out of gas! How do they not put enough gas in their tank? Seems kind of stupid..."

I wasn't irritated. It was just confusing to me.

"No, it's because they only put a little bit in at a time so that it doesn't get stolen."

"So what doesn't get stolen?"

"The gas, silly. There are people who steal gas from others."

"How the heck do you steal gas out of a scooter?"

"They use a siphon to, well, siphon it out."

"Oh, huh, didn't realize that was a thing. Well, that's shitty."

No matter where you were, it seemed there were people doing shitty things. And whether it was a matter of survival for them or not, it sucked to have to take these things into consideration so as to avoid being on the receiving end of their shittiness. Thankfully, I was surrounded by some pretty awesome people, and safety was truly not a concern. It was especially helpful that I lived across the street from the bar and did not have to worry about getting home. Plus, the campsite had security guards. I also had Don and Scott who I knew would have my back if I needed help. Stefano too.

————

"Teeesh, I want to make love to you. Please, let us to go home."

He had had a couple of drinks. He wasn't wasted by any means, just slightly sloppy.

"You want to make love to me? Hmm, I'm not sure you know what that phrase really means."

I spoke fast and was laughing when I said it, kind of mocking him quickly because that was the opposite of what happened last night and also because I knew he wouldn't understand what I was saying.

"Ma? What? I'm not to understand, Teesh."

(*Ma* is 'but' in Italian so he often prefaced with this.)

Well, maybe I should be open to trying again. I mean, I really was horny for him. Maybe he'd get me this time. We went back to my tent and tried again. But sadly, it was more of the same. Couldn't he tell I wasn't into it? I certainly wasn't pretending like I did before. Dammit. I was very much in my head about it all while he lay on top of me, thrusting against me like a hammer on a nail.

"Ugh! Ugh! Teesh!"

He was moaning, and I was having a hard time believing this was as good as it was going to get for us. Sigh. Did he really think this was working? I guess I should probably say something or do something... But *what*? Shouldn't we just *know*? Shouldn't we just be totally in sync?

God, this was so fucking disheartening!

the dawny

. . .

"STEFANO, I HAVE TO GO."

"What? What? What you mean?"

It was very early and still dark outside and he was confused and groggy but I didn't want him to wake up and wonder where I was.

"I'm meeting Hendri for a dawny. Don't worry, go back to sleep. I'll see you tonight."

"Ma? Okay, okay, Teesh. Kisses."

And he planted one on my mouth before going back to sleep. I quietly gathered my stuff and met Hendri on the road.

Hendri, a white South African dude, was pretty much a legend around these parts. He was tall, stately, good-looking, and had the kind of crazy sparkle in his eye that your father would never trust and certainly would not want you to be around. You should've seen him at the bar the night before, casually perched atop the open concrete sill, back against the wall, legs stretched out in front of him. He just sat there in the middle of the crowd and waited. He didn't have to do anything at all. He'd just 'be', and one lady after another would come to him.

I 'be' instead of I 'have to be'

"Jesus, he's dangerous," I'd said to Stefano and Leonardo at the time.

Hendri was a shit-hot kayaker and a raft guide, and I'd heard that he'd paddled some of the craziest channels on this river, stuff nobody else would touch. He had that 'I'm not afraid of death' attitude towards life, which made me think he was a bit psychotic.

An hour or so into the night, he must've gotten bored of all the lady attention, or most likely didn't find anything he liked, so he came and had a beer with us. To be fair, it was pretty hard for Stefano to understand anything in a crowded, noisy, music-filled space, so he and Leonardo carried on a convo in Italian while Hendri and I got to talking. I had met him on the river the other day while he was safety kayaking for a raft trip, and he was indeed paddling the river as though he was floating down a stream of trickling water. Dude hardly even put in a paddle stroke, whereas I was flailing around trying my damnedest not to flip.

"Hey, I saw you on the water the other day."

"Excuse me?" I replied.

Surely he was mistaken.

"Yeah, it's not like there's a lot of chicks paddling. You seemed like you had everything under control."

"Oh. Cool, cool. Thanks."

I was literally dying. Was that a compliment? And side note, if that was what he observed, then perhaps I should consider pursuing an acting career. In the interest of not talking about me any further, I changed the subject.

"So, you didn't find any ladies to take home tonight?"

It was a safe bet he was trolling for women. He smirked back.

"Nah, they're all Overlanders. Not much fun for me."

Popular among backpackers, overlanders are big trucks that you can travel in... erm, overland. It's a rugged experience, but you can drive across all terrain in them so it was a fun way to explore. This was one of their regular stopovers because white-water rafting + hot raft guides + a bar overlooking the water =

party scene. They would be here one or two nights and then be on their way, but loads of trucks came through at least three nights per week.

"I see..."

"Hey, do you want to paddle tomorrow? Do a dawny?"

"A what?"

"A dawn session."

"Oh, really?"

Wow. I could not pass up on an opportunity for a dawny with this legend, even though I immediately felt nervous enough to want to barf.

"Um, yeah, for sure. Why not?"

He was a curious one. A man of mystery. Of course, I wanted to break that code and was keen to keep talking to him but Stefano was ready to leave.

"Teesh! I'm want to tire. None."

I took a moment to translate.

"Oooh you're tired and want to sleep!"

"Teesh, no. No after 7. No can correct me."

It was true. His English went completely down the drain in the evenings and we had an agreement that I couldn't correct his English after 7 p.m. Made sense. Poor guy's brain was fried by that point.

"Okay okay, we go."

I turned to Hendri.

"So... meet at 5 a.m.?"

"Yebo, see you then."

Yeah-boh meaning yes.

"Cool, bye. Bye, Leonardo!" and threw him a wave before heading home.

And, well, you know how the rest of the evening went.

———

I wasn't actually sure if Hendri would show up or not, but there he was, waiting, talking to Freddy.

"Mornin' bru!"

You know you're someone's buddy when they call you *bru* (South African for buddy or friend).

"Hiii!"

I was both excited and nervous, which I'm sure was overtly obvious with my extra-large obnoxious smile. I really did not want to make a fool out of myself paddling with him, especially since he asked *me* to go. Now maybe this is just me wanting desperately to feel special, but I seriously doubted he asked many chicks to go for a dawny. And before you say anything, I promise you it's not because he was wanting to hit on me. That was not the vibe I was getting or giving. I only had eyes for my Italian.

I turned my attention to Freddy.

"Hey Freddy! You're up early. You gonna meet us at the take-out?"

"Yes, Tish, yes. I'm going to bring Robert too."

"Cool, cool."

And off we headed, down the dirt trail to the put-in. Paddling out to the middle of the river at the dawn of a new day, the world felt at peace. Glassy water, sounds of nature, silence from man. We paddled towards the first rapid, warming up with some backward strokes, forward strokes, waking up with a roll to get wet and ready.

He challenged me right away.

"Tish, not Ribcage, we're going over this way. Follow me."

And instead of heading downstream, we paddled further over to the left to a different channel.

"Um, I don't know this route."

This was no time to let my ego get in the way.

"Yeah bru, you heard of this one, right?"

"Um, Brickyard, is it?"

"That's the one, sweets."

Fuckkk!!! Not only would I not have the familiarity of the usual run, but I'd have to run this rapid blind! The only thing I knew about it was that it had a technical line, which, in other words, meant you don't want to fuck up or else you'd have the pleasure of sliding down a sheer wall of rocks on your face.

"I don't know, dude. You sure about this?"

"Just stay left, then work right. Follow me."

He could obviously tell my nerves were on the rise so he looked me straight in the eye, and held his gaze. He didn't say anything, with words at least, but his intense eyes spoke articulately .

Stop being a pussy. I wouldn't have lured you this way if I didn't think you could handle it. Now wake up to what's in front of you, get your nerves in check, and conquer it.

His look certainly had an effect on me because it straightened me right out. When at the top of a rapid, with the horizon line in front of you, you don't have much choice except to put your game face on. The fear doesn't just disappear, so you consciously have to put it in the back seat, where it's under strict orders to sit still and not say a word. Only courage, skill, and fun can be up front. They can even share the wheel because they come from the same confident vibration. Fear, on the other hand, is maniacal by nature and would only drive you into a ditch and piss everyone else off. A real menace to have on board, that's for sure.

"Okay."

I sat tall and focused. This was not the hardest rapid I'd faced. With so many rivers under my belt by now, I knew I could handle it, whatever it was. Hendri gave me a nod and then, with just a few paddle strokes, disappeared into the rapid. I followed him in and stayed closely behind. It was like a pinball machine, but with a series of steps and little drops, continuously down a 50-foot rapid. There was not a ton of water through this channel so I get why it was called Brickyard. I didn't want to get pushed sideways or else I could hit a rock and flip, so I focused on facing downstream while making micro strokes to the left and right, bumping into small holes but making sure I didn't let anything kill my momentum. It was quick and intense, and I made it to the bottom in a matter of ten seconds, Hendri greeting me with a warm smile.

"See, Tish? I didn't have any doubt."

"Thanks!" I said, somewhat out of breath.

We paddled back over to the right and did the rest of the usual rapids, thank God. Having conquered that first rapid, my confidence and adrenaline were pumping, which made me feel super relaxed for the rest of the trip, even surfing in some of the waves on the way down.

The main rapids done, we linked up to one another, holding the side of each other's boat, and cruised towards the take-out, letting the river do all the work while the mist rose off of the water and the early morning dew evaporated, as if the earth was presenting itself to the day. We came upon a fisherman in a log canoe. As we began to drift past him, he called out to Hendri:

"I want her."

Hendri did not respond, nor did I. Was he joking?

"I want to marry her," he yelled out.

This time, and without hesitation, Hendri responded.

"Nah, you don't want this one. She can't cook, she can't clean. Nah, this one's no good…"

"I want her," he yelled again.

As we left him in the distance, I was thoroughly confused while Hendri was chilling as if nothing had happened. Obviously, I had to ask.

"Excuse me, um, what was that? What just happened? Was that for real?"

"Of course it was," he said matter-of-factly, though his smirk was not lost on me.

It was shocking. The culture here was barbaric, in terms of women being like property used to fulfill the needs of men. I mean, the fisherman directed his attention at Hendri, as if Hendri could sell me off. Not to mention I'm not even referred to as a woman, simply 'this one'.

To know and then to *experience it first hand* are two very

different feelings. I wondered what the women here felt. Did they know they were oppressed? Did they question the way things were?

We got to the takeout, hopped out of our boats, and took a few minutes to chill on the shore and soak up the peace, listen to the birds, spot some monkeys, and quietly appreciate this beautiful morning paddle. The fisherman was the only other human soul we met, and it felt like we got to enjoy a secret that nobody else got to witness. It was just ours, for us, a perfect moment in time.

**rise with the sun
get wet—have fun!
wash your worries away
and let love rule the day!**

After a few minutes, I broke the silence.

"God, I love Africa!"

Ugh. Cringe. Even as it was coming out of my big fat mouth, I knew it was an ignorant comment. Africa is vastly diverse. Beautiful, of course, but also full of chaos and darkness and pain and suffering.

"You know, this is not *all* of Africa," he responded.

He was a man who had been on many an expedition throughout the continent. He'd seen political strife and poverty and God knows what else. From what I'd heard, he was not afraid to walk the fine line between adventure and death. I felt like such an idiot. He didn't know I'd traveled from Kenya down to South Africa on my own a few years ago, so to him I was just another tourist basing my sentiment on this teeny tiny little oasis. At least, that's what I imagined he was thinking.

We picked up our boats and began our hike up the hill to meet with Freddy and Robert.

———

That night, after Stefano finished thrusting himself into me once again, he asked, "Teesh, you like it like that?"

I definitely didn't have the energy to pretend, so maybe he sensed something.

"Um, well, not so much..."

"Eh? Teesh, I only do that way because I think you like!"

"But do you like it that way?"

"No! I mean, is okay but I don't mind other way!"

Well, this was taking an interesting turn.

"Why you not tell me, Teesh?"

"I don't know!"

But I did know. I was scared to say how I felt. Why, though? It was just sex. Maybe I was afraid to lose him. Maybe I was more concerned about pleasing him. Isn't that what we, as women, are trained to do? Maybe it was time I expressed myself a little more. If he could manage to do it with his basic English, I certainly could up my brave.

"What you like, Teesh?" his voice was gentle now.

He leaned over and kissed me softly with his plump, sexy lips. My heart felt it deeply, vulnerability immediately following. But I also felt safe. Safer than ever. I wanted so much to open my heart to him even though I wasn't quite sure how. I'd have to try. I'd have to do something.

"I like the way you kiss me," I said, feeling shy.

I pulled myself next to him, so that our bodies were touching.

"I want to feel your body next to mine," I continued.

I began feeling for the zipper of his pants...

"Ma, Teesh... But wait, wait..."

"Wait?"

What's happening? Oh no, what have I done?

"Is okay. Relax! We go slow..."

"Oh, sorry."

Fuck. I was rushing into it. Damn, I was nervous.

"Teesh, we just to feel the love talking..."

Somehow, he made complete sense.

"Breathe, Teesh… I am to make love to you…"

He wrapped his leg around mine, put his hand on my back and gently pushed me up against him. His tongue slipped into my mouth and he kissed me with every wet bit of it. He was good. I loved kissing, our tongues an appetizer, wetting our appetites for the main course. I felt a rush of energy moving throughout my body as we slowly undressed. I licked his hairy chest, his nipple, his belly button, his cock. He flipped me on my back and entered me. That feeling, that rush, this time we were in sync, our bodies intertwined, connecting, moving as one.

"Mmm," he moaned, "Teesh."

I surrendered to him. I let him in completely. I let myself feel him deeply, emotionally, lovingly. He was gentle, then strong, slow, then fast. He read me better than I had ever read myself. He was in the right places at the right times, listening, feeling, moving with me and to me while the swirling of energy kept building within me, tears now quietly rolling down the sides of my cheeks as I felt love in a way I'd never felt before. And when I could not wait any longer, I moaned and groaned and came for what felt like an eternity. He did not hesitate to come with me, our climax an unraveling of sexual tension and frustration and fear and loathing… all of it, all of the pent-up emotions that had been trapped inside my body my entire life exploding out of me like a firecracker.

I had felt Heaven. It was the most glorious feeling in the world.

> **may you experience the juiciness of this life**
> **let it burst from your soul**
> **and drench you from head to toe**
> **go ahead and taste its sweet nectar**
> **filling you with love as you go!**

Stefano. *Definitely* my Italian lover.

an invitation

. . .

I HAD ALWAYS WONDERED if those insanely sensual love scenes in romance movies were sorely exaggerated, setting us up for expectations that could only ever disappoint. For the most part, I'd say that's true. But now I can also confirm that with the right person, in the right moment, it's absolutely possible.

The next couple of months were divine. Stefano and I, despite a few hiccups, were still very much on point. His English continued to improve, while my Italian did not, though I can't say I put in much effort. I nursed him through his bout of malaria, while he did *not* nurse me through a night of drunkenness and falling off a boda boda.

"Teesh, ENOUGH!!"

He was not impressed.

I also learned that his last name was Goia, which means 'joy' in Italian, and the name of his hometown was Laino Borgo, located in the Calabria region of Southern Italy.

The fun I was having wasn't just about him, but about the community as a whole. I had become friends with kayakers who came from all over, and found a tight-knit family in Stefano, Leonardo, and Pablo. Life was good, the days casual: wake up in my tent with Stefano, have tea or coffee with him before he'd have to gear up for a day on the river, have breakfast with Rudy, my new campsite neighbor, then out for a paddle with Scott and Don, usually meeting up with others sporadically along the way, have a lazy afternoon chatting, napping, or playing frisbee, meet up with Stefano after his day, have sex or not, fall asleep, repeat.

> **no need rush or bend**
> **to the silly constraints of time**
> **didn't you know they're only a distorted dream in**
> **your mind?**
> **so relax. don't delay!**
> **release the stress of the day**
> **by going outside for some play!**

I learned that Hendri was notoriously elusive, sometimes super chatty at the bar and other times mysteriously quiet. But oddly enough, his one consistency was encouraging me to run Itanda, a Class V rapid, and some would even argue a Class VI. I had always thought that meant un-runnable AKA 100% death. This was a rapid that very few people ran due to its length and complexity, distance from shore, and overall intimidation factor.

There were three stages to it, yet you cannot properly scout it to get a clear visual or get the landmarks. You also cannot eddy out mid-rapid and take it piece by piece. There was a top section with a couple of tricky maneuvers, a mid-section with a gargantuan hole called The Bad Place, and yet another bottom section with yet another gargantuan hole called The Other Place. Each section is fairly long (say 90 feet), and with the massive volume of water pumping down it, you definitely do not want to swim, especially at the top. A swim would most definitely mean spending a lot of time underwater. Yes, my life jacket would *eventually* bring me to the surface, but it didn't have enough buoyancy to combat the downpull of current in fast-moving, deep-water hydraulics.

In essence, the only way to run it for the first time was to have someone with experience lead you.

I was scared, but I wanted it. Scared, but confident enough. Scared, but thinking I could be ready when the time was right. I didn't know when that would be, but I'd know when I knew. In the meantime, I honed my skills with lots of practice doing Silverback runs, the section of rapids I did daily, and surfing a specific wave that Hendri insisted I surf even though it was big and intimidating due to the ledge shortly below it. Cue the thought: *Don't go there or you'll die!*

The thing with surfing in a kayak (playboating) is you're most likely going to flip over at some point. That's just the nature of catapulting yourself into the air and doing tricks. So you need to be on point with your roll otherwise you're going to go over the ledge and that's just not cool.

Anyway, I trusted in Hendri. Of all the people to be my guide, he was the best of the best. He'd paddled it countless times before and was not intimidated by it. Maybe at one time he was, but at this point I imagined it to be more like splashing around in the bathtub. For me, though, a successful run would be major epicness, and likely the biggest and longest rapid I would ever dare to enter.

———

"Teesh! Teesh! My God, but wait, I want to ask you before..."

"Huh?"

We were in my tent, half-asleep after another tear-jerking round of love-making and teaching him the word 'orgasm,' when he startled me awake.

"Before, em, our orgazzmm… I want to ask for you to come on trip. We will go on two day with clients. I want for you to come."

"Oh, you're doing a two-day trip? Cool! I haven't done the other section. Yeah, of course I want to come with you guys. Sounds fun!"

"Ah yes, Teesh! We for sure gonna have fun!" He kissed me again. "Mm-mm-mm, Teesh. Yes. Orgazzmm."

Then he lay back down and immediately fell asleep.

hendri and itanda

. . .

"TODAY IS THE DAY, TISH."

It was Hendri. I didn't even know he was coming on the trip with us until I saw him at the put-in. I handed my dry bag of overnight clothes to Pablo before responding.

"The day for what?" I asked, pretending I didn't know what he meant.

The thing is I wasn't sure I was ready to hear it. He didn't even need to say the words and I already felt sick to my stomach.

"You know, Tish. Don't play games with me."

Still, I couldn't acknowledge it. I couldn't even look him in the eye, that damn fear mongrel inside me desperately trying to get me to run away. He walked within six inches of me and stared me down. What he said next was so simple, yet voiced with such composure that the fear got up and exited stage left…

"Itanda."

Silence ensued but the energetic conversation between us went something like this:

Me: "Today?"

Him: "Best day ever."

Me: "I see."

Him: "Wake up to it, Tish."

Me: (feeling into my body, listening...)

Him: (staring, waiting...)

Me: (feeling, listening, accepting, until finally, I had words) "Yes, it's time."

Him: (nodding with a wink, a smirk, and holding up his hand to give me a high five before returning to the truck to unload rafts)

you are strong
and oh so fierce
a bright shining star
in this incredible universe

I would be letting the reality of this sink in all morning—calm yet nervous being the two main emotions to manage from the very start, before even hitting the water—but that was okay. I had experienced this many times before. Conquering Phil's Hole, landing in Taipei, hiking Thorong La pass, kayaking in the flash flood in Ecuador. I hadn't been sure I was going to succeed at those and many other moments, but nonetheless I made and committed to them by choice. They were moments to 'wake up to'...

What did that mean exactly? Good question.

For me, it meant to approach the situation with eyes wide open, an acute awareness, and 100% presence. In other words, I didn't want to let doubt creep in and distract me from what I knew I could do. Choosing wisely was the story I told myself.

Yes, of course, I needed the skills to succeed, and I did have them. Now all I needed was unwavering confidence in order to utilize those skills. Remember, giving attention to your nerves makes you rigid, which means you're not loose in the hips and your paddle strokes are not well-directed. You're probably going to catch an edge and flip because that's what you're focused on *not* doing. You see, by focusing on *not* flipping, you're actually visualizing flipping. And you create what you think. A foot too far left or a foot too far right or a not-quite-good angle and you're going over, so you have to have the mind-strength to maintain your attention towards success, so that every stroke can be directed towards a good outcome.

You've got to get in the zone!

———

So far, the day had been perfect, with everything leading up to Itanda going by without a hitch. The weather was perfectly hot and sunny as always at this time of year, the clients were having a blast, and nobody had flipped. On the long flat section before Itanda, I jumped in Stefano's raft and enjoyed the casual conversation of his visiting English clients. I couldn't deny the butterflies in my stomach, but I *could* be distracted by the funny British people with their dirty jokes and zinc-covered faces.

Soon enough, though, the time had come. Hendri paddled up to our boat.

"Tish. You ready?"

I wanted to barf immediately, but managed to play it cool.

"Ready."

"I'll meet you up ahead," Hendri replied, and paddled off.

The rest of the trip's occupants would not be running this rapid. Instead, they would get out at the top, portage the rafts on river right, and put them back in the water at the bottom. This was also where lunch would be happening at a spot where you could actually get a distant view of part of the rapid without trees in the way. I was hoping to complete the rapid before anyone would have a chance to see me.

I got in my kayak, and just before launching into the water, Stefano gave me a hug and a kiss.

"Good luck, my love..."

I could tell he was nervous for me but I could barely acknowledge him. I'm not even sure I said anything before launching myself into the water and paddling away towards Hendri, who was drifting with the light current a few meters ahead. The river at this point was wide, so the current was slow, but at the top of Itanda, it would narrow up and drop in elevation, converging the water into a very long rapid some may call a waterfall. Personally, I would say it was more like a five-tier cake, gradual in steepness.

I could see the horizon line about ten meters ahead. To the left of me was a small rock about the size of a kitchen island. Perched on it was a long-legged, long-necked white and gray bird with a yellow beak.

"You see that? That's a heron," Hendri said with a smile. "It's a sign of good fortune. This is a good day, Tish."

The best I could do was look at him and smile. At this point, all of my energy went into managing my emotions. Hendri, an intuitive giant, seemed to know exactly what I was going through, and gave me exactly what I needed. Instead of a pep-talk, we paddled silently towards the horizon line. His presence helped to steer me in the right emotional direction and I guessed it was no small undertaking to guide someone down this behemoth of a rapid. He would be the one to have to try and save my ass if anything went awry and I ended up swimming, but even then, there's only so much he could do. In actuality, it would be more like looking for me at the bottom and hoping I was still breathing.

In the weeks prior, we had spent a solid amount of time discussing the rapid in preparation for it. While we couldn't scout it literally, he could at least talk me through it. He had even drawn me a map so that I could visualize where I needed to be at certain times, describing each tier of the rapid. The only question was: would the hand-drawn map translate to real life?

We were ten feet away now and I was about to find out.

what it means to wake up

. . .

HENDRI TURNED AROUND and gave me a final 'good luck' with a slight nod of his head and I noticed a bright sparkle emanating from his wild eyes. Then, while still drifting backwards—*poof!* —he disappeared over the horizon line. Crazy motherfucker.

> **I see a spark in your eye**
> **go ahead…let your dreams fly**
> **it's safe to be in the clear**
> **and completely free from your fear!**

Now it was my turn. As I came upon the horizon line, everything around me—the roaring waves, the singing birds, the whistling wind, even the obnoxious voices in my head that I was working so hard to ignore, all of it—suddenly fell silent as if God had hit the 'mute' button on the world.

I dropped into the rapid, relieved to spot Hendri about eight feet ahead of me. Yet even with his presence and guidance, I felt so alone. It wasn't a bad alone, simply an alone in the knowing that this was all on me. It was up to me and only me to pull myself through.

The moment of truth had arrived.

With laser focus, I honed in on the line ahead. We paddled from river left to river right, the first six-foot-drop in front of me. *Go over it straight, Tish,* I told myself. *Dig your paddle in.* Whoosh! Down the slide I went... Nailed it, but holy fuck, that was bigger than I expected. Tier 1 done.

The channel opened up slightly but the water was still pushing fast. *Stay alert and on point.* Next were a few smaller drops and two smaller holes that were not to be discounted, because 'small' was relative. They were only small in comparison to what I knew was yet to come.

Hendri was not far in front of me, facing upstream to see where I was at, not even putting in a stroke, like he was on a kiddie's ride while I was over here on a gigantic roller coaster about to fly off its tracks. He turned around for the next section: Pencil Sharpener. This was Tier 2, a diagonal hole I needed to be close to, but just narrowly miss so that I could ferry behind it and get further right to avoid... *Fuck!* I got too close and clipped the corner of it—rookie mistake—but I braced with my paddle and caught myself from flipping. *Good save. Let it go. Stay focused. Ferry. Turn.*

And then, there it was staring me in the face, a full-frontal view of The Cuban. Terrifying. This was Tier 3. A 40-foot-high and 40-foot-wide hole. *Here we go.* I paddled to the right, the water fast and furiously wanting to suck me in. But no, I learned my lesson with Phil's Hole and this was a similar maneuver. I had had a bird's eye view from the top. Now as I paddled past just to the right of it, I was getting a worm's eye view. It was a perspective that only a handful of brave people before me had chosen to experience, and now here I was, carving out this moment in time just for me. Nobody else could share it with me, not even Hendri, because he was already past it. It was a humbling sight to behold, a real David and Goliath experience.

The world around me, on all sides, was one giant Herculean tornado of water. Yet I managed to tap into the order within its chaos. The next gargantuan hole, The Bad Place, was just ahead. Tier 4. Coming out from under The Cuban, I was now riding back up the rollercoaster to its next peak. I had lost Hendri by this point, which was not surprising at all. These waves were full of personality, constantly in flux. He could be anywhere. I came up to the top of the peak and for a split second I could see his orange kayak in the distance. *Focus, Tish. Be here now.* I put myself in third gear and ferried to the left, dropping quickly down this massive ride, and successfully avoiding The Bad Place.

Now for Tier 5, the final push. It was imperative to keep my wits about me because it wasn't over yet. Again, I had to paddle right to avoid The Other Place, but after that, I couldn't remember what I was supposed to do. By the time I was at the peak and staring into its jaws, well, it didn't matter what I was supposed to do because it was too late and I was heading straight for the center of it. *Not good.* I had lost my focus for a split second and now I was about to be swallowed whole.

Desperately seeking a way through, I saw a tongue (green water moving downstream , which is good) in the middle and I remembered now that, yes, I had to go through the middle, and pray. It's a surging hole which means you won't know if you're going to hit it when it's green (meaning it'll push you right through) or if it's white (meaning aerated water, a recirculating hole). Here I was having to give it all up to the gods. *Go figure.*

I straightened up to give myself the best chance of punching right through it. I dug in with a solid stroke and held my paddle in the water, hoping it would grab the water and pull me through. At the last second, the line opened up for me and—*blup!* —I sailed right through without any pushback.

It seemed the gods were with me.

Woohoo!

The hardest part was behind me and I could relax as the waves got smaller and smaller in front of me as the river widened back out. I had made it! I had successfully run Itanda! It felt like I had gone through a portal and come out the other side.

Hendri paddled out from an eddy he had been waiting in (where he was also probably praying I would emerge upright) and he was all smiles. I could hardly believe myself. Had I really just done that? He came up to me and, our boats now side by side with our paddles resting on the edges, leaned in and gave me the biggest congratulatory hug. I was in a state of shock and awe. It was both the longest and shortest moment of my life. Like it took forever but was also done in a flash. I looked up at Hendri, amazed at this man who had faith that I could run this rapid, encouraged me to do it, *and* guided me down it. With the largest smile on my face, there were only two words to sum up how I felt.

"THANK YOU!"

"Congratulations, Tish. You killed it!"

I was on cloud nine—an expression I'd heard plenty of times and had always wondered what it really felt like. This had to be it, 100%. We paddled to shore, him as enthusiastic as I was, and just like that morning of our dawny, the two of us got to share another secret moment in time, a moment I'll never forget.

Paddling as silently as when we were at the top of the rapid only a few long minutes ago, everything felt different now. While paddling towards the horizon line, I know I said I was keeping my emotions in check. And I was. That's the thing about having to keep your emotions in check, though: it means they are there, wanting to be heard. That's the fight-or-flight response of our autonomic nervous system kicking in. Yet I knew in my heart I was going to dominate. And even if it did all go drastically sideways, I also knew I was unlikely to die. I may have been traumatized and gasping for air, humbled and probably humiliated... but I would most likely have survived. Now I was at the bottom. Nerves were replaced with relief, even glory. I had come out the other side unscathed. I had done my job and I had done it well. It was not perfect, but it was perfectly good, and that was enough.

I was a warrior, a victorious warrior.

winding down from the ultimate high

. . .

"TEEEEESH!!!"

Surrounded by green leafy banana trees, Hendri and I followed the short trail up to the top of the hill and emerged onto the clearing at the lunch spot. Stefano must've spotted us immediately because we had barely shown our faces before the dark-brown Italian had thrown his arms around me. Well, he was trying to at least, but our life jackets were making it kind of difficult to get the reach around.

"My God, Teesh! You are okay! You did it? You are good? How was?"

He was cupping my face now and kissing me all over like an excited puppy.

"I try to see you but just one moment of your head... your helmet..." Stefano said.

"Oh, you saw me for a second but just my helmet?" I repeated.

It was bright red and easy to spot.

"Yes, yes, Teesh, my God I'm to worry. You are okay?"

"Yes! I'm okay! I did it, Stefano!"

Wow! Let's just say, I was feeling very special, very loved. But also very thirsty...

"Ste, I need some water, please."

"Ah okay, Teeesh. Come, you drink. I must to help with the food."

He walked with me to the cooler of juice where I chugged about three cups while he went to help with lunch. My adrenaline still pumping, I needed to take a step back and calm myself down. The day was not done. There was still an afternoon of rapids I had never paddled before and I needed to have energy for it. With a cup of water in my hand, I stood and stared at what I could see of the rapid. The view of Itanda was much different from this distant sideline. It was crazy how in just a few short minutes I had gone from gladiator, battling it out in the middle of the Colosseum, to spectator, admiring the ginormous set of rapids from a distance.

"Girl, you are my hero!"

I turned around to see who was talking to me. It was a client. She was strikingly beautiful with long white-blonde hair and a bright, happy smile.

"Oh wow, thanks!"

"That looks like the scariest thing in the world, but girl, I saw you, like a star in the grand sky! Your boyfriend was yelling and running and trying to catch a glimpse. Isn't he the sweetest thing?"

From what I could tell, she had an American accent from the South, like from Alabama or thereabouts. We chatted for a bit which helped the adrenaline to stop pumping so hard. I managed to eat some lunch, reveling in my accomplishment while enjoying the fresh pineapple and barbecue chicken served under a basic thatched roof. The guides were busy making it all happen, but Leonardo and Pablo managed to come by and congratulate me and give me big hugs.

"Chichileo, Tish!"

High fives and pats on the back and smiles all around. I really did love these guys.

Shelly, the client I'd just met, and I ate some food and admired the old and giant monitor lizard in front of us. Apparently, he was a frequent visitor and obviously not afraid of humans. He was six feet long and 200 pounds with an intimidatingly long neck and claws. Think Komodo dragon, because it's basically the same thing. We were told not to get too close, because, well, teeth. And yes, venomous, but not to humans. Still, nobody's trying to get bit by a dragon.

The afternoon section went as smooth as could be. When we arrived at our camping spot, I was elated to have completed the day so successfully, though, it was all still sinking in. With the build-up to Itanda (like weeks of prep and all the nervous energy from just thinking about it), and then it taking all of three minutes, well, it's over so fast it's almost like it never happened. That part of it was weird, but now I got to enjoy reveling in the aftermath. I would enjoy it as long as the energy was still here.

I helped set up camp and prep dinner. Like in Nepal, there was a lot of sharing stories around a campfire and getting to know the guests and laughing at all the strange and misunderstood conversations that occur when you're with two Italians, a Costa Rican, a South African, and now a southern gal from Alabama, some crazy Brits, some other quiet ones, and me, the Canadian. We were in fits of laughter throughout the evening, though less and less made sense as the night went on and the beers became empties. Most notable was Hendri cozying up to Shelly, an unsurprising hottie match made in Heaven. They, of course, disappeared at some point during the drunken debauchery.

As the small crowd slowly dispersed and people stumbled into their tents, Stefano and I stayed up a little while longer to watch the sky, the stars, and revel in the absolute perfection of the day.

"Thanks for looking out for me today, Stefano. I was so happy to see you after Itanda."

"Teeesh, my love, you are magnifico."

My God. My heart. He squeezed me tight. I felt him. I felt his care, his kindness, his big heart. I squeezed him tighter, and felt our love intertwine.

My heart had been blown wide open by this guy, so much so

that I hadn't even realized how closed off I'd been until I felt the warmth of love coursing through my veins, softening my attitude. He wore his heart on his sleeve, loving me openly and tenderly which had been slowly melting my shield of armor. I wondered why I was so on guard. *What was I afraid of?*

"I love you, Stefano."

I didn't think twice before saying it. It was just as natural as could be.

> **imagine a romantic relationship that goes**
> **beyond 'I'.**
> **where truth and hope collide**
> **a vision to behold via your mind's eye**
> **a dream no longer 'mine'**
> **this is love divine!**

My Italian lover in Uganda, a truly magical experience.

a new light

. . .

WE AWOKE EARLY the next morning after only an hour or so of sleep. Truth be told, after I told Stefano I loved him he practically threw me over his shoulder to carry me back to the tent where he proceeded to ravage me like a hungry animal. It seems he had waited patiently to hear those three particular words, and once they reverberated into his ears, I tell you it was like he was let out of a cage. I have never been licked in so many places.

We made love, and we fucked.

At times he pumped me hard and I liked it. I wanted him as deep as could be and there was no shame in our vocal appreciation for the ecstasy of mind-blowing heart-opening sex. We fucked soft, then hard. I licked him. He licked me back. My pussy was wet and his cock was wild and we had not a care in the world. We moaned and groaned, and at one point I swear we both roared.

I'm certain even the animal kingdom was impressed.

I had hoped everyone else was too drunk and passed out to hear us. When we emerged from the tent, I hoped I wouldn't be met with a bunch of high fives or winks or anything that would confirm we had had an audience.

"Nice one, Tish!"

Okay, never mind.

"Girl, you were giving Hendri and me a run for our money!"

It was Shelly.

"Oh my god, I'm so embarrassed. Wait, no, I'm not! That was by the far the best night of my life!"

"And day, for that matter."

"Best 24 hours ever!" we said in unison.

"BEST DAY EVER!"

It was Hendri, passing by us with a wink.

"And you?" I asked Shelly.

"Don't you worry about me, darlin'. I'm fine as hell!"

I'm sure this verbal exchange was the equivalent to the high fives I saw the guys giving Stefano out of the corner of my eye, which I pretended not to see. Besides, it was time to get back to work. There was too much to do with packing and getting on the river for Day 2.

Total Vengeance, Hair of the Dog, and Kula Shaker were the names of the main rapids to get through, and now that I had my big run out of the way yesterday, my mind was clear and I was able to be more available to the trip should anyone flip. Which, thankfully, nobody did. We finished off with Nile Special, a fun wave aptly named after the local brewery in Jinja, the town at the mouth of Lake Victoria where this famed kayaking region began.

I pulled up to shore at Nile Special, where we stopped for a quick snack and juice, but when I pulled my sprayskirt and began hoisting myself out of my boat, a large frog jumped out too! But that wasn't all. Next came a fucking rat! *Jesus Christ.* I never thought to check my boat before I got in it this morning, and thank fucking God I did not feel either of them while I was mid-rapid, because I'm sure I would've freaked out and pulled my sprayskirt and ended up swimming. I promise, you could not make these things up.

After our snack and after rinsing out my boat and double

checking for other critters, it was time to move on. By this point, it was a mostly flat water paddle the rest of the way. Everyone was in great spirits at the take-out, a successful trip for everyone involved. We loaded and deflated the rafts, followed by all the gear, and finally ourselves. We rode in the back of the truck, clients inside, sun on our faces, satisfaction in our minds, and love in our hearts as we traveled down a bumpy dirt road for two hours back to base.

I spent much of the time lying down on the gear, watching and admiring Stefano as he gazed out the back, or made broken conversation with Shelly who was having the best, most light-hearted time of all. As a photographer and philanthropist, she was not afraid of adventure, and had traveled many places solo for work. She was definitely someone to admire, and I was glad to have a woman along for this ride.

Weathered and exhausted and finally back from our two-day adventure, I felt like a new woman. I had accomplished a majorly intimidating goal that wasn't even on my radar until only a short while ago. Remember when Phil's Hole was an intimidating goal? Ha! Now it felt like a minor speed bump of a rapid compared with what I just did!

And lo and behold, I had unexpectedly fallen in love. I'm honestly not sure how I felt about that phrase, though. Do we really 'fall' in love? I *felt* love. That's more like it. I let it in, in a very big way, and it felt fabulous.

Two major milestones for this kayaking trip, I'd say.

> **a glimmer of light**
> **with a side of slay**
> **is a lot like magic...**
> **wouldn't you say?**

I met the boys and Shelly at the Explorers bar to enjoy some drinks and food while admiring the red African sky as the glorious sun set over Bujagali Falls. We were all in a state of quiet awe, celebrating one of those picturesque moments you want to last forever.

But nothing lasts forever.

Little did I know that change was just around the corner, and my little oasis was about to crumble.

everyone's leaving

. . .

"TEEESH PLEEEEASE, I must to talk with you…"

"I know, I know, I'm sorry. After she leaves, I promise."

Stefano had been trying to get my attention since the day before, but I had been preoccupied with Shelly who, sadly, was leaving that afternoon. The truth is, while I enjoyed being surrounded by all this male energy, it was a nice change to have Shelly around. I liked our girl talks, which were mostly about boys, namely Ste and Hendri, and with her upbeat and charismatic personality, she was the perfect addition to our eclectic little family. She and I had become fast friends in the three weeks following Itanda and I was not in the least bit happy about her departure.

"Shelly, I'm not okay with you leaving me."

I was helping her pack up her tent, which was making it all too real. I hated this. First Red Fran and now her. Damn, who was going to be next?

"Oh darlin', I hate it too, but I've got to get my tush back to my mama to help her with her move."

"I feel like I should take priority over your mother…"

I was kidding. Sort of. Jesus, I used to be so good at this letting go business. What happened to me?

"But seriously, aren't you going to miss us?"

"I'm gonna miss you like the devil misses his pitch fork…"

I gathered this to mean *a lot*.

"…but we're friends forever, sweetheart, and I'm never gonna let you be anything less, no matter how far apart we are."

She had a way of making me feel special, like my existence was important to the survival of the planet. Maybe that's why I liked her so much. In any case, Pablo, Leonardo, Stefano, and I were all there to hug it out, sending her off on the back of Hendri's motorcycle while she left a trail of southern magic in her wake.

Stefano: "I'm to miss her."

Me: "Me too."

Stefano: "She was good for you."

Me: "Huh? How?"

Stefano: "You smile a lot with her."

Me: "She's funny."

Stefano: "Ma, I don't think I understand a lot, what she is saying. Ma… but… when she talk, and you smile… I smile. Is enough for me!"

He put his arm around me and we walked to The Black Lantern for a date. Just the two of us. God, I could eat him up and swallow him whole.

———

"Are you serious?"

This couldn't be happening, could it?

"And you never thought to mention this before?"

Now I knew what he wanted to talk to me about, and I hated it. I got up from the table, knocking my beer over in the process, its contents spilling out as hard and as fast as the tears spilled down my cheeks. Stefano was following directly behind, his hands no doubt flailing about while trying to explain himself. But I was all out of sorts and spinning like a chicken with its head cut off, veering left, then right, not knowing up from down, tripping my way down the dirt road and back to my campsite.

"Teeeesh! Wait! Ma, but... wait!"

> **I walk with you to and fro**
> **though sometimes it's just in circles we go**
> **we face our fears head on**
> **making new waves all along**
> **oh my God what an adventure we're on!**

I unzipped my tent and practically fell into it. I tried to zip it up behind me but Ste was right there, launching himself in before I could shut him out. Great. I wanted him to fuck off and leave me alone and yet I also didn't want him to fuck off and leave me alone. So I did the only logical thing. Nothing. I said nothing and did nothing. Well, that is unless you count flopping onto my Therm-a-Rest and weeping uncontrollably like a fool who realized she never should have let her guard down.

"My God, Teesh, I'm stupid. I'm sorry. I'm not to know you have this... I... ma... ugh."

His English disintegrating by the second, me unwilling to come out of the metaphorical hole I had dug with my head into the mattress, it was obvious to both of us that conversation was out of the equation. There was not much left for him to do except lie down beside me and hold me while I wept.

He was leaving.

Stefano, my Italian heartbreaker.

———

At some point in the longest, most miserable night of my life, I must've fallen asleep, because I awoke the next morning so puffy-eyed I could barely open my lids. As much as I felt hurt and betrayed and wanted to run far away from him, I couldn't help but cling tight. I was at complete odds with myself. My open and vulnerable heart had suddenly turned into a deep and gaping wound.

Maybe I was being too dramatic. But was I?

Stefano was already hovering over me, his distraught exposed by the lovingly concerned look on his face.

"Teesh. Come, please, we go to eat. And talk."

One thing was for sure, I needed to get out of the tent and get some air, and he clearly wasn't going anywhere yet. Not that I wanted him to, either. We walked in silence to the Treetop Café. It was your typical thatched-roof structure, except this one was on wooden stilts. We walked upstairs and I collapsed on the old couch. The 'kitchen' was just a small space in the corner with a blender, coffee pot, camping stove, toaster, and mini fridge. Unlike one of our regular dinner places, which was just a couple of guys cooking over a one-burner stove outside a small, dark hut with a couple of wobbly tables and tree stumps for seats, this place was new. It had a lovely view with an even lovelier breeze. It did not match my mood at all this morning, but seemed to slightly calm my nerves. Ste sat tight next to me, our bodies touching, his arm around me, a silent comfort to balance out the emotional hurt.

We drank coffee and ate toast, and finally Stefano began explaining himself. Last night, all I had heard was that he was leaving, and now I was learning why. He had to go back to his hometown to start the season for the rafting company there. It was his company, as a matter of fact.

"But why didn't you tell me before?"

He was leaving in one week, and it felt deceptive to have withheld that information until now.

"Ma, Teesh, I'm not to understand. I tell you I have company many times. I'm sorry is a… a… surprise?"

Was I having a major brain fart? Apparently, I was so lost in la-la-land that I didn't think to anticipate this, even though, now that he was explaining things, it shouldn't have come as such a shock.

It was April. Of course he needed to go home to get ready for the season in Italy.

"And, ma, Teesh, you were to leave too, no?"

Truth be told, even though my year was just about done, in my delusional mind, I would stay here forever with him. I was such an idiot.

"Teesh. I am just for us to be happy now. I want to enjoy, not to think of the tomorrow."

The blow was definitely softening.

"I guess that makes sense…"

At least, I wanted it to make sense. Desperately.

"Please, Teesh, I'm just want to love you. And you to love me."

He was staring into me with the eyes of a man who loved deeply. I knew this because I couldn't ignore how I felt it in my soul. Still, I couldn't just let go of my hurt so easily.

"Well, I could come to Italy with you…"

I was grasping, and he knew it. Sensing my inner chaos, or rather, desperation, there was a long pause before he finally said something.

"Is okay, Teesh, not to worry right now."

I wondered what he meant by that.

"So, you don't want me to come? I mean, it's just an idea but we can make it work. Or I could just meet you there later!"

A plan was already beginning to formulate in my mind, but Stefano was not meeting my enthusiasm with his own. Instead he was silent, his energy flat as he searched for the right words.

"Ma, Teesh, please, I think… better to keep our love here. Do you know?"

"Um. I don't know. What do you mean? You don't want to see me again? Wait… Are you breaking up with me?"

I could feel myself begin to panic a little bit. Was my Italian lover done with me?

"Teesh, I think better to keep our love here. Life is crazy, you know? I don't want to force a plan. This… this we have here is beautiful, natural…"

Fuck. He *was* done with me. My eyes widened with surprise, shock. As reality set in, my head lowered, those same eyes now hiding behind their lids.

"Oh. I see."

"Teesh, you not to worry, ma, please! There is more for you, more heart to open. I know this."

I was frozen in time. The silence was deafening and I was forced to be still with it instead of reacting like I normally would, hurling hurtful words as an attack in my defense. There was nothing for me to grab onto here, so the silence filled the void.

Minutes passed like this, Stefano ever-present and loving all the while.

"Please, Teesh. Is not bad… Is not, ma… What is the word… re…?"

"Rejection?"

It came to me easily because I was feeling it so hard.

"Si, si, Teesh! Not the rejection. Is only love. Please!"

If not for his words, and his vibe, I doubt I would've allowed myself to be understanding of his perspective.

> **from then until now**
> **through the ups and the downs**
> **we sure didn't know how it was going to work out**
> **but we knew in our hearts**
> **we could trust what we felt**
> **believe in this love**
> **and explore our true selves**

I understood, because I could feel it. Ste hadn't done anything wrong or bad. And even though my heart wept, I couldn't fault him for not wanting to ruin the moment by telling me he was leaving. If I were honest with myself, I might have done the same thing in his position. Maybe he was worried it wouldn't be the same in a new environment and didn't want to jinx what we had, like the way it ruined things for Dusty and me.

Like the Annapurna Circuit, I will power through this, I decided. Stefano took my hand as we left the Treetop Café.

"Teesh, come, let me make love to you."

It was hard to believe anyone could break up with you and then turn around and make love to you, but I assure you that when it came to Stefano, he could, and he did.

———

The next week was your typical bittersweet love story of two people attached at the hip. We ate, we drank, and we had lots of sex. We laughed, we cried, we talked, and we said nothing at all. The intimacy was as breathtaking as the sunsets over Bujagali Falls, which we admired every evening. I loved it, yet hurt over it at the same time, trying to stay in appreciation of it while also being pestered by a question that kept lingering in the back of my mind. I swatted at it incessantly, but like a mosquito it just kept coming back to torture me. *Where had I gone wrong that he could so easily leave me?*

Finding peace during this time was more challenging than running Itanda.

> **every moment a new opportunity to breathe**
> **to wear your heart on your sleeve**
> **just call upon love**
> **let it help you believe**
> **ask for joy and sweet laughter**
> **now be still and receive**

———

I still wasn't ready for it, but the time had come.

"Ciao, Teesh. For you, always my love. My heart..."

He kissed me and kissed me and kissed me some more, not

afraid of letting his thick, wet tongue moisten my face. I hoped this was not our final goodbye. We'd meet again, wouldn't we?

"You guys!"

It was Leonardo, coming in for a group hug. Then Pablo.

"Chichileo!" he yelled.

"Chichileoeooooo!" we all chorused, while in a tight group hug.

Stefano got into the cab and we watched as it drove off down the dirt road, turned the corner, and finally disappeared. I hung out with Leonardo and Pablo for a little while longer, all of us feeling the change in energy. In sticking to my original plan, I had two weeks to go until returning to Canada. I'd need to find a way to adjust, but Stefano was a solid piece of a wonderful group dynamic, so this would take some time. As adventurers, we were all familiar with changing dynamics—the one constant in this nomadic lifestyle. Even so, some change was harder than others and this was a loss we all felt.

After a few beers, I said goodnight to the boys and took a boda boda back to my campsite. It was strange to be alone again. Not lonely—at least not yet—but alone. I unzipped and crawled into my tent, and there on the bed was a card and a present. The present wasn't wrapped. I picked it up and held it in my hand, admiring a very pretty matching bone bracelet and necklace made, I would guess, by a local artisan lady. The card was hand-made paper with a small painting of a Ugandan tribesman made, again I presume, by another local artist. I stared at it, wanting to savor the moment, tears already streaming.

I could only read it for the first time once, and knowing how special the words would be, I stared at the art on the card for as long as I could, waiting, anticipating.

Finally, I took a weeping breath and opened it.

JINJA 4/4/1999 H12,00am

Hi Teesh , for shure I'll not have right words for saying what I would to say...you know my english!!!

But, at the same moment, I think I seyd many things with my eyes and my hands...

I'm gonne miss you a lot...

But I'm going to leave my soul around yourself, then when you will feel sad, alon, you

have just to think about me whit all the energy you have...

I will be there!

I Love you...

Stefano

I fell onto my Therm-a-Rest and wept. Even in breaking up with me, his love was strong. Even in leaving me, his love was strong. *How is that possible?* I wondered. I would read this card a million times over in the years to come, and each and every time, I would weep just as hard as the time before. How could I not, when it was all I had left of him?

time may come
and time may go
but the love you give
will never grow old

be the light

. . .

A MOTHER'S comfort goes a long way. I was glad I was already living at home when I received the news…

I had returned from Uganda seven months earlier, at the end of April, completing my year abroad. I'd skipped the season in the valley, opting instead to live in Toronto for the summer, because I was out of money and needed to save up in a big way. My logic was that if I went back to guide on the Ottawa, I would still be broke come fall, and that would leave me no options for winter travel.

I was currently working at Sporting Life, a big sporting goods store just a few blocks from my house. Surprisingly, I was also enjoying it. Not so much the part about selling clothes, but the atmosphere and the people I worked with had good vibes. I hadn't saved as much as I'd hoped to by now, but living rent-free at my parents' place was a big help.

"Tish, why are you being so hard on yourself?" my mom asked.

Unfortunately, I had recently received some heartbreaking news and things had taken a nasty turn for me emotionally.

"I just… I just wish I had done a better job of…"

She interrupted me before I could finish. I think she was sick of watching me mope around like I had been for the last few weeks.

"It's like you're punishing yourself, but for what? You did the best you could at the time, so why not accept it for what it was instead of for how you wish it could have been?"

That was all fine and logical, and it's not like I didn't want to feel better because I did, but...

"Because I miss him, and I'm never going to see him again, and I just wish I had done a better job of loving him."

"From what you've told me, it sounds like he loved you with all his heart and that he also felt *your* love, otherwise he wouldn't have spent all that time with you. I know there's nothing I can say to make you feel better, but you can still continue to love him, and know that his love, his light, will also *always* be there for you."

I hadn't shown her the card, but she was spot on about that. It would forevermore be a constant reminder for me to love more openly. But right now, I was having a hard time with that. I was stuck in the past—wishing, wanting, hoping to wake up and realize, to my relief, it was all just a bad dream. Because Stefano had... he had... I struggled to say it, even to myself.

Stefano had drowned.

He was raft-guiding in Chile when it happened. I didn't know the details, except that his raft had flipped in a rapid and he had got stuck somewhere. Was it under the raft? A rock? Leonardo had dug around for some info, but nobody really knew.

The news of his death floored me. We had had a couple of letter exchanges since my return home. We had a friendly, happy exchange, though I admit my heart still hurt and I missed his presence. He had only been in Chile for a couple of weeks when it happened. His second letter to me was to tell me that he was headed there for the rafting season and I could tell by his wording that he could barely contain his excitement.

Teesh...I am to go to Chile! Can you belief? It very fast, this action. I not have many time to write, I think, because of the place. But I would to try!!

These place a dreem to go. I am so much joy!

I am hope you to be good, my friend. Happy and loving all the life!!!

Kisses,

Stefano

My Italian lover, dead? It didn't make sense. It wasn't fair. He didn't deserve to die.

"Tish, I know words don't teach, but I will say this. He will always be a beautiful lesson in love, and eventually, with time, it will be easier to think of him and feel all the joy and love you gained in knowing him instead of feeling the pain and loss of losing him."

> **look up when you're down**
> **take a bow—surrender to the now**
> **feel the love in a frown**
> **let go and allow your world to turn upside down.**

Since my return, my parents and I seemed to be in a better place, more appreciative of one another. I guess all that time away with little contact forced us all to mature.

"But what do I do now?"

It was a somewhat rhetorical question because I knew she couldn't tell me what to do about this grief. *She* knew she couldn't tell me what to do, either.

"You always seem to find your way. There's no rush, Tish, you don't have to *do* anything right now."

My dad came into the kitchen and did the unexpected.

"Aw, Tish, I hate to see you so sad."

He put his hand on my shoulders and gave a little pull on them. A profound moment of affection.

"Thanks, Dad."

That's the thing about my parents. I know they were always there for me when I need them most, no matter our differences in opinion. Man, I was learning a lot about love.

Given my confused state of mind, I needed the stability that traveling couldn't provide, so I stayed at home and continued to work at Sporting Life over the holidays. It was good to be smothered by all that Christmas spirit: walking home from work in the freezing cold with snow-covered streets, all the lights on trees and buildings, being greeted by a warm fireplace, baked goodies, and the comforts of home. I hadn't been here to experience this in years, and appreciated the ridiculousness of it all. My New Year's was mellow, opting to stay at home which matched my quiet and reflective mood.

By mid-January, my heart had warmed a little, while the rest of my body was getting a painful recollection of why I always escaped winter. I was constantly freezing. Hot showers and workouts at the gym were my only reprieves from the bitter weather. Having saved enough for a plane ticket and some budget travel, at this point I couldn't help but imagine thawing out in some tropical haven. It didn't involve kayaking, though. Nope. After the traumatizing news of Stefano, I realized how fortunate I'd been over the years. I seriously could've died multiple times had it not been for sheer luck and/or timing. I was done with whitewater for a while.

This time, I wanted something less dangerous with a little less equipment. Something easier. Perhaps a retreat where I could learn to surf? And dance? Definitely a place with good food... And a place to heal my heart.

I pondered over it, imagining what *it* felt like, but not knowing what *it* was. I didn't have the brain capacity to seek anything out, so I just dreamed. And kept dreaming.

"Hey Tish, this is Luc..."

Apparently, the universe had heard me loud and clear, because two weeks later at work, my manager's friend walked into the store. He had just returned from a place that sounded exactly like what I had been envisioning in my mind. I could hardly believe it. But as he spoke, a deep, automatic inhale came upon me, just like it did that time I opened the River Run pamphlet at MEC (Mountain Equipment Co-op). I had to trust it. For the first time in months I knew that everything was going to be okay.

I knew, because my broken heart could feel this was *it*.

I was inspired.

> **nothing is wrong**
> **and everything's right**
> **so get out of your head**
> **and come back to the light**

———

Did you enjoy this book? Please consider leaving an honest review on Amazon so that others may enjoy it too! It makes ALL the difference in the world for a small indie author to garner as many reviews as possible. We need that cred! **Scan the code to go straight to the review form for the book.**

Want to know what happened to Red Fran after she was stolen? Great! **You can grab it at: www.tiffanymanchester.com/pack-light-bonus-epilogue. (Wait! There's more on next page…)**

travel inspo - resources

For more info on the Maasai culture:
http://www.maasai-association.org/maasai.html

For facts on Nepal:
https://www.adventurewomen.com/blog/article/did-you-know-fun-facts-about-nepal/

https://www.facebook.com/WorldsAmazingFacts/posts/the-kali-gandaki-gorge-nepal-worlds-deepest-canyonthe-kali-gandaki-gorge-or-andh/1033006666827910/

https://en.wikipedia.org/wiki/Kali

Handling Death: The Dynamics of Death and Ancestor Rituals Among the Newars of Bhaktapur, Nepal ~ by Niels Gutschow and Axel Michaels

afterword

the 4 minute feelgood pick-me-up

It's time to hear what LOVE would say
and feel the kindness it would have you know
but how can it ever lead the way
when you're so afraid to let go?

surrender your mind
go ahead and lose all control
gladly watch those struggles fade away
they can't help you in any way.

there's no need to fight back
so give it up
be okay with caving in
go ahead, let go of everything
but this…

allow yourself time to go ooh amazingly slow
as you gently release any need for control

let feeling good
be your one true guide
and only move forward
when you feel it inside

listen for a whisper
your heart beats the way
divinely entangled
cannot lead you astray

have faith in what's true
ask the angels to play
they want you to laugh
can't wait to brighten your day

you were born to feel good
know every day drama free
live your life so on point
others can't help but see.

all you've got is the present
so Let the past go
take care in each moment
true Love is the goal

now listen for answers
let god show the way
he'll give you bright signs
clear the path for your way

so drop all that baggage
to lighten your load
be free from all pain
it's the only way home

believe in your truth
and watch your life thrive
forget about the how
keep your eye on the why

you're ready
let go!
and Be glad to surrender
...you know...
forgiveness is the answer

your mind can change
you'll have such happy days
when you follow the feelgood
you'll break all those chains

you've got it in you
we're all in this together
we share the same truth
just be still - remember

about the author

Tiffany Manchester is a new adult fiction author and surfer. She is also a former professional athlete, four times National Champ and a Bronze World Medalist in the extreme sport of freestyle white-water kayaking. Before the glory of the professional scene wore off, she spent a decade traveling to remote places around the world on a shoestring budget, seeking the thrill of epic adventures on mountains, rivers, and jungles. Eventually she found herself embarking on a spiritual journey in Hawaii, one that introduced her to meditation, dance, magic mushrooms, angel tarot, and of course, surfing - and began the creation of Follow The Feelgood®, a simply system for tapping into one's intuition to make guided decisions with ease.

One night years later, she met a beautiful man on the dance floor of an electronic music festival. Still based in Hawaii, they have no kids or pets, enjoying instead the freedom to sleep and travel as they please.

Find her at: www.tiffanymanchester.com

Printed in Great Britain
by Amazon

13025419R00141